Did she realize on mortality?

Achilles couldn't make eye contact with her. His ears strained and he heard the ebbing pace of her heart. What surprised him was that she hadn't needed to sleep in the earth to complete her transition the way most vampires did. The mutated virus in her system was odd indeed.

"Stop spoon-feeding me, Achilles. Just tell me how to stop whatever's happening," Beck demanded, interrupting his thoughts.

"You can't stop it. Your senses are becoming amplified. Sight, smell, hearing, taste...are amplified a thousandfold."

She leaned forward. "What about touch?"

Unable to stop it, his gaze flicked to hers. "Yeah. That, too." She stretched, hands high over her head, causing her neck to arch and her breasts to thrust proudly forward. Gods, she was gorgeous. Gorgeous...dangerous....and completely off-limits.

Books by Theresa Meyers

Harlequin Nocturne

*The Truth About Vampires #107
*The Vampire Who Loved Me #113

*Sons of Midnight

THERESA MEYERS

Raised by a bibliophile who turned the family dining room into a library, Theresa has always been a lover of books and stories. First a writer for newspapers, then for national magazines, she started her first novel in high school. In 2005, she was selected as one of eleven finalists in the nation for the American Title II contest, the *American Idol* of books. She is married to the first man she ever went on a real date with (to their high school prom.) They currently live in a Victorian house on a mini farm in the Pacific Northwest with their children, a large assortment of animals and an out-of-control herb garden. You can find her online at her website, www.theresameyers.com, on Twitter at www.twitter.com/Theresa_Meyers, or on Facebook at www.facebook.com/TheresaMeyersAuthor.

Dear Reader,

Welcome to the second story in my Sons of Midnight miniseries. When I first met Achilles Stefanos in *The Truth about Vampires,* he was merely a friend of the hero. Dr. Rebecca Chamberlin was a friend of the heroine in the same story—a slightly sarcastic brainiac, who buried herself in her work. Together they were utterly wrong for each other (on the surface), which made them perfect to shake up each other's world. One is shut down emotionally by choice, the other by circumstance.

As a writer, I usually create a soundtrack to inspire my writing. For me, "Wake Me Up Inside" by Evanescence solidified Rebecca and Achilles's relationship because it perfectly captured the essence of living as a halfling vampire. If you'd like to find out other songs on the soundtrack, stop by my website at www.theresameyers.com.

Theresa Meyers

For friends,
no matter where they are and how they change.

Thanks to my tea friends
for your support and friendship—
Karla Baehr, Jennifer Hansen, Rachel Lee,
Kendra Lutovsky, Diana Burko and Dorina Potz.
You girls are the best.

To Ed Trask
for reading and encouraging me
to get the book done.

And Jerry,
because you've been more than my husband,
you've also been my best friend.
Thanks for all you do to make my writing possible.

Chapter 1

Everything Clan Security Commander Achilles Stefanos had learned over the last few centuries told him that she was trouble. Gods, he got no satisfaction knowing his instincts were right. He was screwed. Well and truly screwed, and not in a way he'd have appreciated.

Remaining invisible, he perched on the window ledge outside the four-inch-thick windows of Genet-X Laboratories, scoping out a sterile white lab. Anyone glancing out the window would see only the top of Seattle's Space Needle against the last glimmers of a bloodred sunset. He watched as Dr. Rebecca Chamberlin lowered her rectangular black-rimmed safety glasses and rubbed at the worried expression on her forehead. Her wide, expressive hazel eyes narrowed as she peered at the row of small vials filled with a swirling dark greenish black liquid were in front of her.

Vampire vaccine. At least that's what he'd heard from very reliable sources. It seemed that she was a sort of genius freak when it came to anything biochemical and specialized in genetic engineering. Her curly auburn hair gave her heart-shaped face an even more youthful appearance. Too young and far too pretty to come up with something so potentially threatening.

Even through the glass, his ultrarefined senses smelled the glossy coating of cherry balm slicked over her full lips. She stretched, hands over her head, giving him a peek of her curvaceous breasts beneath an aqua-colored T-shirt and an open rumpled white lab coat. She hardly looked like the super brain he'd been told to watch by his clan's *Trejan*.

She looked more like a sweet diversion, the kind of woman that vampires aspired to make mortal playthings. Exactly the kind of mortal he would have picked if he had the time and inclination to indulge himself. A curl of desire started low in his belly, rippling into a full-blown flame. He forced his libido to take a hike. *Focus, solider. Focus. She's merely an objective. Another mortal.*

She was smart *and* beautiful, which meant she was even more trouble than his team had anticipated. *Beware the enemy dressed in silk.* The words of his Spartan commander echoed across the eons thumping like a war drum in the back of his skull. Once a warrior, always a warrior. Never surrender. Never retreat. A Spartan's duty, balanced with a Spartan's curse—to live forever and never die in battle. Gods, what a sorry mess.

Itching to act rather than sit and observe her supple curved form, Achilles focused his attention on the wind blowing in from the water. Ozone from an incoming storm rolling across the Pacific tainted the breeze. He shifted his weight and rubbed his hands over his cropped dark blond hair, causing it to stick out in tufts and spikes. Not that it mattered. This decade's fashions encouraged the messed-up look, and he always did his best to blend in with the mortals. It made his efforts in providing security for the clan so much more effective and had helped him survive when others had not.

A buzzer sounded in the room, causing the beautiful doctor to cross over to the security panel by the door. What he wouldn't have given to be her lab coat, brushing against her derriere.

Is that your report? The voice of Dmitri Dionotte the clan's *Trejan,* and second in command of the Cascade vampire colony, interrupted his thoughts.

No. Merely an observation of the objective.

Her looks are immaterial. Tell me about the vaccine.

Our sources were correct. The vaccine is being created. Do you wish me to intervene and stop their work?

No. Continue to monitor the situation.

Sure. Why not. He was only standing on a window ledge six stories above the ground like a bird of prey. *I'm on it.*

Achilles. There was a long meaningful pause. *You can be on it, I just don't want you in it. You are not to make contact with the researcher unless absolutely necessary. Any kind of contact. I'm saying this as both your* Trejan *and your friend. There's a rumor that if she begins to transition into a vampire because of her work with the virus that you'd be selected as her mentor. You don't want to start anything physical with this woman.*

Got it. Right now, as far as I'm concerned, she's still the enemy. Achilles realized that if the council was once more willing to trust him with a female fledgling to mentor, he'd finally overcome some of the stigma attached to his reputation for the last three centuries. Not that the stigma was undeserved. It was. But he'd already paid dearly for his lapse in judgment and he was ready to move on.

He just prayed to the gods that his new female fledgling wasn't Dr. Chamberlain.

She was temptation enough, damn near his idea of a perfect woman brought into mortal form. As her mentor, he'd be linked to her for eternity—and never allowed to enjoy her. Forever together, eternally apart. In other words, total hell.

"Access code?" Rebecca said into the speaker mounted onto the wall, interrupting his thoughts.

Another feminine voice, the tone more clipped than Dr. Chamberlin's, answered. "Vanquish."

The doctor pressed a code into the panel, her fingers elegantly long, her nails practically short. Had he been mortal, he'd have needed surveillance equipment to see exactly what she'd pushed. Being vampire had advantages, not the least of which was the ability to telescope his vision. His ability to move more quickly than any mortal made her rapid hand motion appear ultraslow to him. One-nine-seven-zero-six-two. He filed the information away and focused his senses on the people entering the lab.

Dr. Chamberlin stepped back a pace, nestling both her hands at the base of her spine. "Good evening, gentlemen." Her lips curved into a welcoming smile. Inside him an unfamiliar interest flared to life. Gods, she had an incredible mouth.

The three older men, two far stouter than was healthy for them, and the third painfully thin and tall, all nodded their greetings to her. They were followed by a slight young woman with dark hair shaped in a severe blunt cut. Where Dr. Chamberlin was all lush curves, the other woman was harsh angles.

The portly man with a shock of thick white hair, an impeccably tailored suit and a telltale black-and-white collar about his throat reached out to shake Dr. Chamberlin's hand. The scientist's hesitation was imperceptible, lasting the space of a mortal blink and at odds with the warm smile gracing her lips, then she stuck out her hand to reciprocate. Interesting. Perhaps she didn't like these newcomers any more than he did. Which wasn't much.

"Welcome to our laboratory, Cardinal Worcher, Reverend Evans, Pastor Snyder."

Cardinal Worcher stepped forward, his hands clasped

behind his back as he surveyed the laboratory. "Dr. Rutledge tells us you've made substantial progress on the vaccine." Achilles couldn't stand hanging out on the ledge like a common pigeon any more. He phased himself through the wall, maintaining his invisibility, and sat down in Rebecca's office chair.

Dr. Chamberlin nodded at the cardinal, her voice holding the excited shimmer of a kid being handed a highly anticipated toy. "I think we've finally discovered the site in the plasmid that has allowed us to perform a cassette mutagenesis and ultimately alter the genetic material for replication."

"In plain English, darlin'?" the shorter man drawled, his brown suit a little more rumpled and matching the sparse brown hair combed over his shiny head. "I'm afraid all that scientific gobbledygook is a bit much for my congregation to understand."

She stiffened, the reaction imperceptible to everyone in the room, but Achilles. The light sweet throb of her particular heartbeat kicked up to a dull roar. If he'd had blood running through his veins, it would be running hot and fast as he listened to the rapid syncopation of Rebecca's heartbeat. His mouth watered.

Achilles stifled the elemental push as his fangs begged for release. Gods, he wanted to mentor a female again, but not *her*. Please *not her*. He shook his head. It was a nonissue. She wasn't transitioning—yet. At this moment she was merely an enemy, an objective. A damn feminine, sexy one. And still very mortal.

* * *

Beck tucked her hair behind one ear and tried to shake off the feeling that someone, other than the three investors, was watching her. Clearly she'd been putting in too many hours at the lab to get this project off the ground.

"Sorry, Reverend Evans." She focused her gaze on the short man with the Southern drawl. "The easiest way for me to describe it would be that we've found the chemical key to unlock the padlock that holds the two chains of the vampire virus together. Now that we've got that key we can open that padlock, take off the part of the chain that makes it permanent and substitute it with the DNA chain we want to render the virus useless. No more virulent capability. No more threat." She glanced at the other men. Perhaps she needed to make it even simpler for them to understand. "Anyone who's been turned into a vampire against their will can return back to their human state in less than a week."

"Theoretically," added Dr. Margo Rutledge with a slight sniff. Beck stifled her desire to do bodily harm to her fellow researcher. Up until now Margo had been quietly gung ho on the project, putting in just as many late nights as Beck had. The other woman had seemed excited about how close their research was to finding a viable vaccine to combat the vampire virus circulating in national blood supplies. What was up with her sudden shift in attitude now, especially with the primary investors here in front of them?

"What do you mean theoretically?" Pastor Snyder's

tight and edgy tone matched his thin frame and severe black suit. He looked like more of an undertaker than a prominent pastor of a church with tens of thousands of members. "We've given your company an awful lot of money to fund this research, *ladies*. We expect concrete results to battle this scourge of evil polluting our nation's blood supplies."

Beck's ire ratcheted a notch higher. Why was it that people thought that science had a miracle ability to speed up time? Research took time. Results took time. Results you planned to unleash on the public, well, that could take years.

"What Dr. Rutledge meant to say—" Rebecca threw Margo a cool glance "—is that we're at the stage where testing can begin. With a few clinical trials on actual subjects, we should know if our approach has been successful or if the formulation needs adjustment to improve the results." At least that better be what Margo meant.

Beck's good friend Kristin Reed had told her from the outset that she suspected Margo had a jealous streak in her. Beck had chosen to ignore Kristin's comment because she'd never seen anything to substantiate it. As a scientist, she didn't believe anything without proof. Four degrees, two of them doctorates in the sciences, had given her that view. As a woman, she didn't believe in judging the path others took until you had walked in their sneakers. Being the illegitimate daughter of a computer industry billionaire had taught her that. She'd lived her whole life having assumptions made about her and she wasn't about to do it to anyone else.

As far as she had observed Margo was competent, smart and hardworking. More importantly she was in tight with the megachurches and religious power brokers that formed the base of their primary research funding.

Beck refocused her efforts on producing a reassuring professional smile for Pastor Snyder. His thin lips had disappeared into a flat line bisecting his long face at Margo's comment. "We should be able to solicit for study subjects by the end of next week," she offered. And doing that would be a minor miracle in itself, not that she needed to reveal that to her uneasy investor. These men were only interested in one thing—results.

Reverend Evans clapped Snyder on the shoulder, the blow pushing the thin man forward slightly so that he had to readjust his footing, his expression turning even more dour. "We're going to need somethin' sooner than later, darlin'. Folks are mighty upset about all this vampire business. With those monsters on the loose, our followers want reassurance that they can seek protection from such damnation. Ain't that right, Snyder?"

"I don't see why you haven't already begun testing the vaccine," Snyder muttered, picking an invisible bit of lint from the flat black lapel of his suit jacket.

"We certainly understand your concern," Margo said, clearly trying to soothe his agitated state. She pulled at the crisp edge of her white lab coat sleeve. "But the government has certain regulations we must follow when testing an antiviral drug such as this before it can be released to the public."

The cardinal lifted his chin looking down his long straight nose. "This is of far graver concern than any flu virus. Vampirism is just as much a physical as a spiritual danger. Certainly the normal process can be bypassed for such a pandemic concern."

Beck eyed the trio of men before her. "That is our plan, of course, Cardinal. Once we have conclusive evidence that our formulation is effective, we'll try to fast-track its approval for the public."

"But, darlin', are you certain it'll work?" Reverend Evans asked.

Beck snatched up one of the vials from the test tube rack on her desk and held it out in front of her. "We believe we've found the key." Inside the vial the liquid agitated as if responding to their conversation, the swirling of dark green never seeming to mix completely with the black liquid around it.

"How is it administered?" Snyder leaned closer, a glint in his eyes.

"With an aspirator shot," Margo said. She lifted the stainless steel apparatus that looked like a high-tech gun from the future. The device had a small metal compressed-air cylinder attached to it. "The vial is inserted in the chamber here and a shot of compressed air forces the drug through thousands of microcuts in the skin directly into the bloodstream through this attachment."

"May I take a look at that?" Snyder asked, his hand extended to Margo. She handed over the aspirator gun.

"And you say the vial goes in here, kind of like loading a rifle cartridge?" Evans asked pointing at the small vertical cylinder atop the aspirator gun. Margo nodded.

A look passed between the three men and Beck barely had time to assess the situation before the cardinal had a firm grasp on her, pinning her arms against her sides.

"What are you doing?" Margo sputtered. "Gentlemen, you must stop!"

"Unless you want to be the next trial subject, I suggest you step back," Snyder threatened, his tone tinted with an edge of hysteria. "We're running out of time on this project and we need results now. If your reputation is deserved, then there should be no harm in you testing it yourselves." Margo stepped back, her eyes wide and frightened as they swung to meet Beck's.

Beck struggled against Cardinal Worcher's hold on her, but he was far stronger than she'd anticipated. Evans grabbed a vial from the rack on the desk and shoved it into the aspirator. Snyder rucked up the sleeve of Beck's lab coat exposing her pale skin beneath.

"If it's as safe as you ladies claim, then we'll be that much closer to a cure." Cardinal Worcher's words were so close they burned Beck's ear.

The cool metal of the aspirator stung as it touched her skin and suddenly it chuffed a loud blast of air. Beck felt the recoil of the aspirator as it bumped against her from the force of the compressed air, but no pain from the injection. She and Margo had purposely sought a way to administer the drug that didn't involve needles since they thought it would encourage more people to try the vaccine.

Worcher released her and she stumbled back from him, yanking her sleeve down over the injection site. A strange warmth began to stream up her arm, like a trickle of heated water slowly moving along her skin toward her heart. Her head started to swim. A whiff of something that smelled a lot like rosemary briefly tickled her nose.

She gripped the edge of her desk for support, shock rocking her system, and suddenly felt as though someone was holding her up, which was strange since her legs seemed to be growing weaker by the second. She still had the oddest sensation that there was another person in the room with them, watching her every movement.

Clearly her shock and fatigue was leading to paranoid delusions. She shook her head and tried to focus on the physical sensations assaulting her system, cataloging them, organizing them, so she could tell Margo after their investors left.

"How long do you estimate the vaccine will take to produce immunity?" Worcher asked Margo as Snyder set the aspirator down on a nearby countertop.

It took a few minutes for Margo's mouth to work again as she glanced from the aspirator to the trio, to Beck and back again. "About two weeks, if it works," she rasped, her voice hoarse.

"Then we'll be back in two weeks to check on your

progress," Snyder said without a trace of concern in his demeanor.

Evans glanced over his shoulder at Beck, his pupils a bit dilated, perhaps by fear at the realization of what they'd done. "She's looking a little peaked. Why don't you just let us out and see what you can do to make her comfortable, darlin'."

Shock was brushed aside by indignation. *Jerk. You're just as culpable as the other two,* Beck thought with venom.

Margo crossed the room stiffly, like an automaton from a freaky fifties sci-fi flick and punched in the access code. The laboratory door swished open and their investors left the room without so much as a goodbye or wish for good luck.

Inside Beck seethed. *How dare they. How dare they do this to me!* Her heart pounded harder, dispersing the drug more rapidly through her system. *Calm. I need to be calm and rational. Think like the scientist you are.* But detached observation was damn hard when it was your own body being used as the lab rat.

While she didn't believe her life was in jeopardy, injecting a subject without their consent was unconscionable.

The door shutting in Margo's face seemed to snap back her research partner out of her shocked state. She hurried toward Beck, her pupils shining with what looked like unshed tears.

Margo's hand trembled as she extended it, then quickly withdrew it before actually touching Beck.

Great. Now Margo was freaking out. One more thing to put on her I-sure-as-hell-don't-need-this-right-now list.

"Holy cow. Oh, Beck. I had no idea they'd do this. I mean Pastor Snyder has been pushing hard and so has Cardinal Worcher, but I had no idea they intended *this*."

She tried to breathe through the heated sensation increasing in her bloodstream and the loud pounding of her heart in her ears as she stared at Margo. "Maybe they didn't. Maybe they just saw the opportunity and took it. Either way, it's not your fault."

"What do we do now?"

"Start taking notes." She gave Margo a weak smile that she didn't really feel, but it was the best she could muster at the moment. "The research must go on, right?"

"How can you say that after what they've just done?"

"Because I wasn't researching for *them*. I started this project to help others like my friend Kristin and my mother who got turned into vampires without their consent." While Kristin had undergone the change as a last-ditch effort to save her from death, her mother had chosen it over her. She knew that now. All her life her mother had relied upon someone stronger to sustain her and in the end it had backfired, ultimately costing her mother her life. Until the truth about vampires had been uncovered by Kris in her investigative reporting, Beck had thought her mother dead.

Now she knew better. Her mother had simply turned

her back on her because Beck had been too needy. Beck couldn't fathom that. She'd purposely fashioned her life so she didn't *need* anyone. Even now, deep down, she hoped that if she could find her mom again, she might be able to bring her back—enough to have a relationship with her again. For a second Beck's chest constricted with memory. She swallowed hard against the uncomfortable lump in her throat. "So you damn well better be taking fantastic notes." She took in a deep gulp of cool air, smelled that damn odd taint of rosemary and swiped at the curls tightening along her damp hairline.

Margo bit her lip and nodded. She rushed to get Beck a chair, then headed for her desk and sat down in front of her computer screen, the light from it making her face eerily bright in the gathering darkness.

Beck relaxed into the chair and tried to describe everything she felt, how the injection had worked, the increasing discomfort and sensations building in her body. She tried to remain detached, an observer of herself. It was like a rapid case of the flu without the screwed up stomach. She left out the paranoia and the odd rosemary scent, chalking it up to her own shock or an odd side effect of the vaccine. After fifteen minutes she felt so tired she couldn't continue.

She slumped in her seat, letting the back of her head rest against the chair. "I don't know about you, but I'm going to lie down. I don't feel so great."

"Do you want me to take you home?"

"Yeah."

Margo came over and slipped an arm around her back,

but the darkness gathering on the edges of her vision was still growing. "Margo." She leaned heavily on her friend, a wave of instability washing over her as she stood.

"Yes?"

"I'm gonna pass o—"

Chapter 2

Achilles stayed invisible and right by her side until Margo had driven an unconscious Rebecca home and tucked her into bed before leaving. The doc looked vulnerable, too damn vulnerable. She was still mortal, for now, which put her firmly in the enemy camp as long as she was working on the vaccine.

While it normally took a mortal being nearly drained to actually begin the transition process, in this case something was different. Her pulse was strong and healthy, making the smooth pale skin at her throat move with a regular even rhythm that drew his gaze. Whatever the good doctors had been doing to change the structure of the vampire virus, it had actually made it more virulent.

Even from across the room he could smell the delicate

balance of her system shifting, the distinctive vampire pheromones beginning to cloak her skin and amplifying the scent that was uniquely Rebecca.

She shifted in her sleep, moaning.

He stepped closer and leaned over. Without warning she swung her arms around his neck. Her eyes were still closed, her lashes long and dark against her luminous soft skin, the deep rose color of her lips mesmerizing.

Gods, what he wouldn't give to taste this exquisite woman. This close the scent of her blood pulsed hot and fresh, smelling sweetly of lemon and ginger, causing his body to ache with the need to feed. Gods, her blood would likely taste like a gingersnap with lemon icing. Afraid of bruising her fragile mortal skin or waking her, he tried with the utmost delicacy to pull her arms from around his neck and settle her back into the bed.

Her hold tightened. She was surprisingly strong. He braced his hands on either side of her shoulders and tried to slip his head and neck out from her grasp.

"Why won't you kiss me?" she mumbled so quietly he would have missed it if his ears had been less sensitive. Her eyes were still firmly shut, moving quickly beneath the thin delicate skin of her eyelids. She was dreaming, her brow creased down the middle. He could see the pattern of faint freckles across the bridge of her nose. He had no business being this close to her. He had no business being this tempted by her. And yet he was.

She pulled him closer, bringing his mouth a fraction of an inch from the curve of her lips. Her warm breath brushed his skin, beckoning him, her scent wrapping around his senses and pulling him as sure and certain as the moon pulled the tide.

His arms shook as he resisted. But as desire warred with duty, desire won.

Deep inside of him his reserve snapped.

Flick. Achilles didn't bother holding back his fangs any longer. Damn she made him hungry. But he absolutely would not feed from her. Not with the transition having already begun. Either it would kill her or it would start the bonding process between them. Neither was acceptable, especially with her loyalties in doubt.

Once she had a mentor and had transitioned, it might be another matter.

No, he would not feed. But what harm was there in one kiss? Especially if she were sleeping. It wasn't as if he were consorting *with* the enemy. Hell, she'd never know it was him. It would be all wrapped into whatever dream played in her head.

Screw it. Resistance was futile.

He lowered his head a fraction letting his lips indulge in the exquisite heated softness of hers, taking care not to scrape her with his fangs. She tasted like summer and lemonade—light, hot, sweet and tart, and utterly delicious. His hunger increased.

She moaned, the tip of her tongue brushing lightly against first his bottom lip and then one of his fangs. He sucked in a startled breath, the sensation spearing straight from his mouth to groin as surely as if she'd laved the length of him with her hot softness instead. The moment was both perfectly right and utterly wrong. He shifted away, gently but firmly pulling her arms from around his neck, profoundly aware that one more taste of her would never satisfy the craving quickly building inside him.

He licked his lips, just to sample the lingering sweetness of her and found it augmented by the sweetness of the lip balm she wore. He stepped back, as if the distance would help. What was it they'd said about forbidden fruit being the sweetest? Damn.

He reached out to his friend and fellow vampire. *Dmitri. We've got a problem.*

A moment later a dark curl of smoke filled the corner of the room as Dmitri transported beside him, his former fledgling now a formidable vampire in his own right. The two of them together, shoulder to shoulder, took up most of the space in the small bedroom. His dark eyes, nearly as black as his hair, lingered on Rebecca, now tangled in her sheets. "What happened?"

"They shot her with the vaccine and she's beginning to transition."

"That's impossible."

"Smell for yourself." The unmistakable trace of female vampire pheromones, vaguely like jasmine, lingered in the air. Dmitri raised his chin, closed his eyes and took in a deep breath. His eyes snapped open, his gaze sharp. "Saints. You're right."

"Whatever frankenvirus they cooked up in that lab isn't abiding by what we normally expect. She's transitioning, slowly, but it's started." He had to look away, the sight of her in the bed feeding the fire she'd already started inside him.

Dmitri rubbed the back of his neck with his broad hand. "But she has no maker."

Achilles tried not to snort. Of course that would be Dmitri's concern, given his own screwed up relationship with his maker, who'd seduced him against his will and changed him into a vampire without his consent. "No. No maker. Not one we can identify at least, unless we can tell which vampire donated the initial ichor sample. For now she's a test-tube vampire."

"Then she's going to need a mentor." Dmitri locked gazes with him, a familiar knowing of centuries together, more as brothers than mentor and fledgling, passing between them.

"Yeah." And that was fine with him, as long as it was somebody else. Anybody else.

Dmitri blew out a harsh breath, then clapped him on the back with his thick hand. "Congratulations." Into his other outstretched hand materialized a scroll secured with black ribbon and the official triple-ring, red-wax seal of the council.

Achilles drew back in horror, putting up his hands to ward off what fate had handed him. "No. Take it back. Anyone but me."

Dmitri looked at the scroll and glanced back at him, his too perceptive gaze boring into him. "Kristin and I thought you'd be pleased to hear the news. You've waited all this time for the council to trust you again with a female and you're going to throw it in their collective faces? What the hell is wrong with you, brother?"

He jerked his head toward the sleeping woman, fisting his hands. "Look at her. Just look at her."

Dmitri gazed down at her, then glanced back up at him, his mouth screwing into a mocking smile. "You're smitten with her, aren't you?"

Achilles growled. "I am *not* smitten. Who the hell uses smitten as a word anymore? You need to stop acting your age, brother. Besides we don't know what she's capable of. She's been working on a vampire vaccine. For all we know she may be a danger to us all."

"All the better reason for the head of clan security to watch over her—closely." Dmitri sniffed the air, his eyes growing wider, the grin dropping from his face. "Saints. You've already started."

Achilles turned away, unable to bear the sight of her now that he knew what the council planned for him. "Don't say it."

"You've already marked her with your scent."

"It was an accident."

"But if they discover you've marked her—"

"Then they must not know. Say nothing."

"As your *Trejan,* I cannot approve of this course of action. It will make you miserable, my friend. You know it and I know it. Don't do this. Let me intercede with the council on your behalf. We'll petition for another mentor for her."

He took the scroll from Dmitri's loose hold, fingering the hard edge of the wax seal. "I haven't a choice. If I refuse the call to mentor her, the council will demand to know why. If I tell them why, then I'll be excommunicated or worse."

"Let me help you," Dmitri pleaded.

"Do you truly want to help me?"

Dmitri's shoulders stiffened. "Of course, brother."

"Then keep your mouth shut."

In the dark of the night the cramps started. They woke Beck from her stupor, her body coated in a sheen of sweat.

She didn't remember how she'd gotten home, or even if Margo had stayed or left. All she knew was that it was pitch dark and she hurt like hell.

A rustle of movement, one that sounded foreign in her house, riveted her attention. She froze. "Who's there?" Her voice echoed, unanswered, in the darkness. She panted against the pain radiating out from her chest. Was this a heart attack?

A large shadow appeared, filling her doorway. The outline of a man. A huge man. One with broad shoulders and a lithe movement that told her he was big and strong. His footsteps made only the faintest sound in her thick carpeting as he moved closer to the bed. Beck scooted backward, crablike up against her headboard and reached down, her fingers questing for the smooth hardness of the bat she kept on the floor beside her bed.

"Who the hell are you? What are you doing here? Answer me, dammit!"

A very masculine, very unfamiliar, voice answered.

"If you'd give me a second to get a word in, I could explain."

Despite the pain, Beck catapulted out of bed and rushed at him with everything she had, baseball bat in hand. She swung and swung hard.

He palmed the bat in his open hand liked she'd pounded him with a feather. It should've broken his hand. Obviously this guy had one hell of a pain threshold. She yanked at the bat, but he held it in a solid, unyielding grip. For the first time in her life, she was terrified.

"Oh, shit."

He grinned, his teeth piercing white against the darkness. "That, Doc, pretty much sums up our situation."

Yanking the bat from her hands he tossed it onto the bed, then reached past her and snapped on her bedside lamp.

Beck had to take back her first impression. He wasn't big; he was enormous like a bodybuilder on steroids. His kick-ass attitude started at his black Doc Marten boots, continued with no-nonsense dark skin-hugging denim and topped off with a black leather jacket over a thin black cashmere sweater. The dark clothes underscored the golden tone of his hair and set off the most intense green eyes she'd ever seen. A shadow of stubble outlined a sensual mouth and a stubborn jawline.

But what completely bowled her over was the power that seemed to vibrate in the air around him like an aura. It was something she'd only seen before when observing big cats, a fierce wildness that seemed to linger just below the level of awareness. Total ego. Total control.

"I'm Achilles Stefanos, a friend of Kristin's." He dipped his head in a nod, never taking his predatory eyes from her. "She was worried and asked me to check on you."

Beck's brain managed to bounce back into gear long enough to form a coherent answer. Her mother and her best friend had been turned into vampires without their consent, and ever since she'd discovered a virus was the key to vampirism, she'd been doing everything she could to find a way to get them back to normal. "If Kris was so worried, why didn't she show up herself? Just wait till I call her—" Beck's knees suddenly wobbled as a wave of heated pain tore through her stomach. She groaned, pressing a fist to her midsection and collapsed back on the bed.

"How bad's the pain?"

"On a scale of one to ten? An eleven."

He made no move to touch her, merely stood there looking at her and crossed his arms, his feet braced wide. "It's going to get a lot worse."

She became ultra aware that this sexy stranger was fully clothed while she wore nothing more than her aqua T-shirt and underwear. She shifted, giving a vicious yank to her comforter and covering her bare legs. How would he know? She didn't even know what was going on. No one could.

The virus was a precisely engineered mutation, something that didn't just pop up as part of natural selection. What was happening to her? What could she do to stop it?

Fear added to the increasing pain. His words seemed to finally filter in past the rush of thoughts in her pain-addled brain. "What do you mean that's not the worst? This is miserable."

"You're about to get hungry. Far hungrier than you've ever been in your entire life."

Her hands wrapped around her waist as she tried to contain the gnawing pain in her belly. Waves of nausea flooded her body and her skin was slick with sweat. "Great," she managed to say, pressing her forearms deep into the pain. "Just the news I didn't want to hear."

Belatedly Beck realized that Mr. Big-as-a-mountain-and-über-sexy wasn't planning on going anywhere and her sad current state wasn't making her the best of hostesses at the moment.

He held out his cell phone. "Want me to call Kristin?"

"I doubt you'd be able to reach—" He pushed a speed dial button and handed her the phone. Ever since Kristin had been turned into a vampire with a nocturnal schedule, she hadn't gotten to spend much time with her best friend. Glancing at the window, she noticed moonlight slanting in between the slats of her miniblinds—so it was night. Kris might still be awake.

Regardless, Kris was going to get an earful next time she saw her. All this time she'd been asking her friend to set her up with someone big, blond and gorgeous and

Kris sends him now? Beck knew by the feel of her unruly hair and rumpled shirt that she looked like hell.

It rang twice before her friend answered. Relief washed over Beck, taking some of the pain with it.

"Are you doing okay?" Kristin's voice was tinged with concern.

She hurt all over but telling Kris that would only make her worry more. "Hey, I've got this blond giant standing in my bedroom who says you sent him."

"That would be Achilles. He's from the clan."

"You sent me a freakin' vampire?" She glanced at him, the size of him, the sexiness of him, the strength of him suddenly making way too much sense. "Why?"

"Beck, he's the best there is and you're going to need it."

"What for? I'm trying to find a cure to get you—" She glanced up at his intently curious green eyes and turned away from him and lowered her voice, covering her mouth with the edge of her hand. "I'm trying to get *you* back to normal, not play for the other team here."

"Just listen to me. We know they injected you tonight with the vaccine you've been working on. There may be a chance you could be turning into a vampire from it."

Beck's heart raced and the pain intensified so that she could barely grit out the words. "No, and hell, no. It's supposed to stop the virus."

"But if it doesn't—"

"It will." She fisted the comforter in her hand. From what she'd been able to discover in her search so far, her mother had hooked up with a vampire, first as his mistress, then as his donor and eventually as an ichor addict. The need for someone stronger than herself to sustain her had become more important than anything or anyone else in her life. Being turned without her consent even if it was by a vaccine was like repeating her mother's mistakes all over again. And she refused to do it.

"Can you please just humor me for friendship's sake? He's an experienced mentor, the best according to my husband. He can make the transition easier for you. Take care of you in ways only vampires know about. Besides, isn't he everything you've been begging me to set you up with for months? Big, blond, rich?"

Beck threw him a cautious glance beneath her lashes. He was definitely the first two. She hadn't talked with him long enough to know about the third one. "Yes, but your timing stinks. I look like death warmed over." Then the thought struck her that vampires were undead and maybe looking like death warmed over had some weird appeal to them. Clearly she was delusional. She shook her head. "Look he can't stay here. He just can't—" The absolute last thing she wanted was for some guy she barely knew caring for her like a nursemaid. But did she have a choice?

Beck forced herself to think past the icy needles of fear prickling her skin, past the pain. She needed to focus on the facts.

Fact one, this mutated virus strain might kill her. And she didn't have the background or knowledge to stop it. Fact two, her friend, who was the closest thing she had to family, until they could locate her mom, trusted this guy—actually had sent him. Fact three, Kris was a vampire. This guy was a vampire. As much as she hated to admit it, if anyone knew what to look for in the signs of a person changing into a vampire, it would be one. Which meant she'd be pretty stupid to send him away, especially since the pain wasn't abating.

"For once in your life, Beck, stop trying to have a game plan for everything and just go with this until we can be certain what's going on," Kristin urged.

Beck sighed. Desperation won out over indignation. She sure didn't want to die, but she didn't want to become one of *them,* either. "Fine. But I'm only doing it as a favor to you."

The tension coming through the phone from Kristin's side instantly relaxed. "That's good enough. Call me if anything changes."

"Sure. Night." She stared for a second at the phone, then handed it back to the stranger in her room.

He took it, scrupulously avoiding her touch as he did so. "You didn't believe that Kristin sent me."

Beck cocked her head to the side. "If a strange man entered your bedroom, in particular a vampire, would you trust his word?"

"No."

"Right. Then cut me some slack." She latched on to the anger burning in her chest formed partly at her own inability to stop the virus and partly at her needing assistance from the very beings she detested. She needed something to help her focus past the pain she felt. She sighed, shoved her crazed curls out of her line of vision and peered intently at him.

He had a thin faded scar that bisected his right eyebrow, the stubble on his chin seemed just as golden as his hair, but a shade darker.

This was the first time she'd really gotten to analyze a vampire up close. Beck had to mentally switch off the scientific section of her brain that was ready to go into full investigative mode. "So you're a vampire, huh?"

"So I've been told." He gave her a playful grin that sent heat spiraling down to her toes. The scent of rosemary that tinged the air changed slightly, now underlined with the smell of warm ocean. If she'd closed her eyes she could have pretended to be on a strip of sand gazing out at the azure water. But there was no way she was going back to sleep with him in her house.

"Look, before we get into this too far, let me tell you that I'm really against becoming a vampire. And I'm not into being a donor girl, so don't even ask. Are we clear?" Of course even as she said the words, her curiosity about him spiked further. Up until now her observations of vampires, with the exception of Kris, had been from as far a distance as possible while she formulated a way to reverse the virus.

Did vampire fangs get in the way when you kissed? Beck wiped her hand across her forehead. Wow. Maybe she was sicker than she thought. There was no way, absolutely no way, that she should even be contemplating kissing a strange bloodsucker, no matter how gorgeous he was, no matter how real the fantasy in her dreams had been before she'd awoken. After all, she reminded herself, no matter how normal he seemed—okay, who was she kidding, he was way better than normal—he was still one of *them*.

"Crystal clear. My only mission here is to protect you and to mentor you through your transition."

"Oh. Good. Glad we got that all straightened out." She finally lifted a hand out to him. "My friends call me Beck."

He grasped her hand lightly in his, then brushed a skimming kiss against the back of it sending an electric arc zinging up her pulse points. "Yes, but I like your given name." His eyes glittered as the pad of his thumb stroked the soft underside of her wrist. "Rebecca...Rebecca... Rebecca." Her name came out a soft, seductive whisper said so slowly, so deliberately, that it sounded like a lover's mantra.

She yanked back her tingling hand. "Stop saying that."

"Your name?"

She fidgeted, bunching the comforter more solidly around her. "It just sounds wrong when you say it like that. It makes me...uncomfortable."

A killer smile lit up his face and made her heartbeat stutter step. "That's even better." He was teasing her.

Beck whipped her body away from him so quickly that a few of her annoying curls bounced, but at least she could hide the tightening points of her breasts from his view. "I'm not sure this mentor thing is going to work out between us. I might need to see about getting someone else."

He chuckled, but it held a sad, hopeless edge to it. From the corner of her eye she watched him crook his finger at a wooden ladder-back chair she kept by her dresser. It seemed to hover across the room and plant itself on the floor behind him. She pulled up the bed covers and tucked them securely under her armpits, then twisted to face him again.

"That's funny to you?"

He smiled in a good-natured way that seemed completely at odds with his ass-kicking appearance, then relaxed back into the old wooden chair. It creaked in protest. "No, it simply shows how little you truly know about vampires. Once you've been given a mentor, that mentor is yours until one of you dies."

Curling her legs close to her belly helped with the pain. It did nothing for the nausea or the growing hunger that had her cramping stomach growl annoyingly. "Hardly likely given you're undead."

He slanted her a mild look. "Precisely."

"So I'm stuck with you *if* I turn into a vampire."

He leaned, tipping back in the precarious chair and propped big booted feet up on the edge of the bed. "That's right, sweetling."

With a sweep of her arm, she knocked his boots off her bed. They landed with a heavy thud on the floor and he arched a dark blond brow at her.

Beck ignored the look then got up and strode with all the confidence she could muster in her semi-dressed state toward her closet where she grabbed a pair of jeans and yanked them on. She glanced at the clock. Five in the morning. With any luck there'd be no one to bother her until 7:00 a.m. and she could make some progress in figuring this mess out before she couldn't think at all. Anything was better than staying here with a massive vampire brooding over her with a gaze that was too intense for her liking. "Good. Then it won't be too long, because I'm not becoming a vampire."

He deliberately placed his boots back on her bed, blocking her path to the bedroom door. "Where do you think you're going?"

She glanced down at his legs, then stepped over them. "To work."

He stretched in the chair, spreading out his arms that had bulging biceps. He managed to take up even more of her bedroom, if that was possible. Then he relaxed. "I'll go with you."

Beck turned and pinned her best no-nonsense glare on him, the one that usually cowed the most persistent interns at the lab. "No. You're not. *I'm* going to work. *You* don't work there."

"Aren't you the least bit interested in playing doctor with me?" He grinned, showing normal, even, very white teeth. The effect of his killer smile would have been devastating to any normal woman. For Beck is was catalytic. She hadn't had a date in so long because she'd been too focused on her research. She'd managed to forget how the air in the room could shift and change in an instant, wrapping around you like a heated blanket when a guy as virile as this was close by. Okay, being truly honest, she'd never dated someone like this. Not even close. Why would she? He was a vampire. Oh, why on earth had Kris sent him?

The intensity of him vibrated in the room. She felt like a hydrophilic molecule to water, helpless to resist him and that sensation took her aback for an instant. She *couldn't* feel attraction to a vampire. After all, look what it had apparently gotten her mother. It wasn't logical. Her common sense scrambled trying to come up with some fact she could fixate on instead of the rush and tumble of sensations crashing around her insides. There was no way she was going to answer his question.

"I thought vampires had fangs." How she managed the words when her mouth was so dry, she had no idea.

He leaned forward resting his thick forearms on the tops of his black jean clad thighs. God, she bet his butt looked spectacular in those jeans. *Snap out of it, Doctor. Remember there's an us vs. them at work here and unless you want to start playing for the other team, you better freakin' pull yourself together.*

"Wanna see?" His eyes glittered.

Beck shook her head pressing her fingertips to her throbbing temples. "Yes. No. I mean I don't need you to show me anything."

"But you're curious." The teasing tone of his voice was seductive enough to make her nipples pucker.

He'd definitely taken her mind off the pain that was lessening now. A dull aching throb she didn't like, but could ignore if she concentrated. "No. I'm a scientist.

Any interest is purely out of a desire to bolster my current research."

He glanced at the platinum Rolex on his thick wrist. "It's 5:00 a.m. I give you four hours, maybe five, max. By then you'll be so hungry you'll be begging me to help you."

Beck huffed and started walking out of the bedroom. She stopped midstep and leaned back past the edge of the doorjamb to catch his intense green gaze. *Ask help from a vampire? Ha! That would be the day.* "You might want to make a note. I don't beg. Never have. Never will. See you." She wiggled her fingers, grabbed her purse and streaked toward the front door as fast as her wobbly legs would take her.

If she'd learned anything from her mother and her own experience as a woman in a highly competitive male dominated profession, it was that a man like that was trouble with a capital, neon-outlined, throbbing *T.*

Chapter 3

Beck made it to the lab in record time and slipped her pass card into the double security scanner, her stomach gurgling loudly. Within these walls, where she'd spent the last six years of her research career, she felt safe and in charge. Unlike home. Especially now that *he* was there.

"Password?" Margo's voice came through loud and clear on the speaker in front of her.

"Vanquish."

The door sprung open and she dashed inside, her heart still beating faster than it should have.

"Hey, Beck. You look…better."

Beck rolled her eyes. "Pfft. I know I look horrible. You don't have to try to make me feel good about it." An unfamiliar sensation skittered over her skin and had her wondering if it was just because she was fighting off the virus, or because Margo seemed a bit cooler than usual.

Margo shrugged. "Shouldn't you still be in bed?"

"Couldn't sleep." She wasn't about to tell Margo that her sleep pattern had been rudely interrupted by a hot vampire who'd offered to play doctor with her. "I want you to take a sample and see what's going on in my blood chemistry."

Margo nodded and went across to one of the large stark white cabinets that lined the far wall and pulled out the syringe and vial to draw Beck's blood. "We should have been taking samples every four hours."

"I thought about that." The stick of the needle didn't bother Beck, but the sight of her own blood trickling thick and viscous into the container made her stomach roll in protest. Yet another good reason why she'd never make a decent vampire.

At least vampire ichor was black. That was easier to deal with.

Margo pulled out the needle and walked away, vial in hand.

"Hey, don't I get a cotton ball or Band-Aid, or something?"

Margo glanced back at her. "Sorry." She brought back both and pressed a cotton ball to the site, then topped it off with the bandage. She capped the vial and stared at it. "It looks a little darker than normal. Perhaps a depleted level of oxygen."

"Let's run a panel on it. I want to see exactly what's

going on and how the altered ichor is reacting now that it's been mixed with human blood."

Margo prepped a sample with dye and slid it under the electron microscope. "Hmm."

"What are you seeing?"

Margo looked up from the microscope, her face blank and remote. "See for yourself."

Beck wedged herself into the chair and pressed the viewer to her face. Under the intense magnification the vampire virus had a distinct hexagonal shape of the bacteriophage with several tail fibers and a collar of whiskerlike projections at the base.

Under normal conditions the bacteriophage would dock with a host cell, and insert the strand of the viral nucleic acid that turned the host cell into a replicating machine, spitting out identical clones to infect the whole system.

In sufficient quantity the vampire ichor contained enough of these vampire bacteriophages, or what she and Margo had come to nickname as vampiriophages, to overwhelm the body and turn the entire system into replicated vampire DNA within less than twenty-four hours. Beck kicked up the magnification on the scope. Yep. There they were. The vampiriophages were still swimming about, attaching to cells in her blood sample.

"At least the metagenetic substitution we made in the virus DNA should stop the process," she muttered to herself. Of course that's what she and Margo had been counting on when they created their provirus.

Beck watched intensely as several of the cells underwent lysis, spilling out a host of new vampiriophages. She sat back with a sick feeling in her stomach.

"It didn't work. The vaccine still isn't viable."

She turned to Margo and met her assessing eyes. A full body shiver shook Beck. It was one thing to comprehend what was swimming around inside her, taking her over one cell at a time. It was another to watch the process happen in the microscopic world of her own blood drop.

Her world teetered, making her light-headed. "I'm turning into a vampire, aren't I?"

"For the time being. But we're close enough to a vaccine that we can still beat it. The virus is acting at a slower rate than normal, giving us more time."

Beck couldn't think straight. "How long do I have?"

"Given the rate of reproduction and the possible protomutations occurring—"

"Margo! How long?"

Margo shrugged. "Maybe a week? Possibly two?"

"Great." Beck worried her bottom lip between her teeth, then had second thoughts about that long-standing habit. She wouldn't be able to do that anymore once she had fangs or she'd be sporting twin lip piercings.

"I can help you pack up your desk if you want."

Margo's comment had the impact of an electric shock— sharp, totally unexpected and completely unpleasant. Beck jerked forward in her chair. "Excuse me?"

Margo turned away obviously unable to meet her eyes

as she pulled a crisp white envelope from the top of Beck's desk and ran her fingers along the edge. "The investors won't let you stay. They've already sent an email to their human resources department earlier today stating that if transformation began to occur you were to be suspended from the project immediately. They think that a vampire, or even someone turning into a vampire, could be a liability on the project. Here's your copy."

Beck snatched the paper from Margo's hand and had the insane urge to rip it in half before she'd even read it. "Bastards. I can't believe they'd do this to me. I should sue."

"I'm sorry, Beck. There's nothing I can do about it."

Well, that was partially true. Margo could have stepped in and taken the shot for her. But nobody would have done that willingly. Beck put her hand to her head. Was she fevered? How was she supposed to figure out a viable vaccine for this virus and stop it unless she had access to the lab?

Margo was the only solution. It was up to her to find the missing link. After all, wasn't that what the investors really wanted—a vaccine that worked? And given that Margo was the only person at Genet-X besides herself who had the highest level clearance on the project, she was the only one who'd understand where they'd failed.

Beck folded the paper in half and stuffed it into the back pocket of her jeans, then turned to put her hands on Margo's shoulders. "You can do something. You can get the PCR primers going and do a site-direct mutagenesis on the plasmid. You said all along that you thought using the PCR method would be the only way to achieve the results we were looking for."

"Yes, but that's going to take a lot more time than trying a different cassette mutagenesis," Margo hedged. "Maybe if we just inserted the restriction enzyme in another site on the plasmid the results would be better."

Beck dropped her hands and began pacing the lab. "Margo, I'm turning into a vampire, a freakin' vampire, against my will I might add, for the benefit of this project. And I'm getting kicked off of my own research endeavor! We don't have the luxury of being wishy-washy about this. Try the PCR approach and keep me informed of how progress is going. I'll try what I can from my end to see if I can find something we missed in the last vaccine."

Margo stiffened. "But what if I get suspended from the project for leaking the information to you?"

"You won't. They wouldn't dare. Not with the amount of money they've already sunk into this. They need for at least one of us to continue, especially after the current vaccine has been proven to be unviable."

Margo shifted her weight uneasily from one foot to the other. "I don't know, Beck. I mean I know you got me the position on this project and all, but this is just too important to jeopardize things."

Beck's stomach cramped harder. Margo's reluctance seemed like a slap in the face, but she totally understood.

After all if their positions were reversed, what choice would she have had? "Don't you think I know that?"

Margo swept her paper-booted foot in an arc across the scrupulously clean floor. "I think you need to go home. I'll work on the PCR option and see if I can make some progress."

Beck huffed, frustration oozing like stale sweat out of every pore. Wait, how did she know what frustration smelled like? She realized that her sense of smell had taken on a whole new dimension, the ordinary scents of the lab had become so pungent they almost made her gag. And there was that strange scent of rosemary that seemed to be a constant presence. A result of the virus? Who the hell knew, but Margo seemed utterly unaffected.

She could have chalked it up to coincidence and been done with it, but then she'd never believed in coincidence. That wouldn't have been scientific. And she'd always placed her faith in the absolute certainty that science could provide the answers to any question if one applied herself diligently enough. Margo was something of an opposite, a scientific mind bent on seeing everything through the idea of a creative force with an ultimate plan. It had made them a stronger team for this particular research project.

As Beck made her way out the lab door and waited for the elevator doors to slide open, the idea of nothing being a coincidence stood out starkly like the brilliant flash from a camera. She reflected on the still frame moments in her mind leading up to her inoculation with the vaccine.

Margo had handled the aspiration injector. She'd explained how to insert the vaccine vial into it and operate it. She'd handed the injector to the investors. And she sure hadn't stopped the men from grabbing a vial and using it.

The whole way down in the elevator Beck's brain spun. All along Kris had pointed to Margo's apparent uneasiness about being the second in the project rather than the lead. Could Margo have brokered a little deal with the investors on the side to skim an extra portion of profits for herself? Had Margo truly believed the vaccine was viable, she certainly wouldn't have needed Beck any longer. And now that Beck, as the guinea pig, had proven their assertions weren't correct the first time out, she got to remain while Beck got the big boot.

Beck rubbed at an uncomfortable persistent itch that was starting at the back of her neck. Coincidence? Maybe. But not damn likely. But then again considering how her life had tipped itself upside down in the last twenty-four hours it could just be a serious case of paranoia.

The doors opened, the metallic hiss louder than she remembered and she stepped quickly through the lobby intensely aware of every security camera as she went. No. Screw the paranoia theory. Heat scorched along her skin. She'd been played. Big time. And her life now hung in the balance.

Chapter 4

Achilles could tell Rebecca was pissed. He waited for her to get into her car, then followed her home, phasing through the outside wall and materializing in a pale blue recliner in her feminine living room just as the front door opened. Maintaining invisibility for long stretches was tiring, and tagging along had done nothing more than gotten him shut down in less time than the two-point-five seconds it took his Bugatti Veyron to accelerate from zero to sixty.

He didn't trust Margo. The thoughts he read buzzing around that busy little mind of Rebecca's had only confirmed his suspicions. If the investors behind the vaccine were willing to sacrifice one of their top researchers in this manner, then they were far more ruthless than he'd anticipated. Even if she wasn't under their direct control, she still would ultimately pursue her goal to change the virus that created his kind.

Dmitri?

Has there been any change?

The backers behind the vaccine research have suspended Dr. Chamberlin. I have a gut. They're looking for a weapon of mass destruction. They want vampires eliminated.

The pause before Dmitri replied to his report weighed heavy on Achilles and prompted him to nudge his superior officer. *Dmitri. You still with me on this?*

I'll report this to the council. We may have to take more drastic actions. In the meantime don't let Dr. Chamberlin out of your sight.

Shall I bring her to the clan headquarters? Being around Kristin may make her transition easier on both her and me.

Achilles shifted in the armchair as he listened for Rebecca's entrance and waited on Dmitri's answer.

It may not be wise to bring her here just yet, Dmitri's voice echoed in his head. *Don't forget until tonight she was working for those who'd be satisfied if vampires ceased to exist. She isn't our ally. Yet.*

I know.

Watch your back, brother.

I thought you'd do that for me, he teased his best friend. Dmitri was the one fledgling he'd guided through transition that he'd become closest to.

I've got a full-time job, Dmitri gibed back. *I don't need another. Just be careful out there.*

He heard a clatter as Rebecca tossed her keys into the ceramic bowl on the small table by the front door. His gaze flicked to the television he was supposedly watching. It wasn't even turned on. With a snap of his fingers, the flat screen burst with color—but the sound remained muted. No need to let her know he'd just turned it on.

She stomped into the living room and threw a glare full of righteous indignation at him. Her hair was a wild tangle of dark brown curls burnished with reddish fire, and the bright pink in her cheeks spiked his thirst. Her pulse rushed with a steady seductive shushing rhythm under her skin. He roughly thrust the idea of how it would feel to sink his fangs into her supple skin to the dark back corner of his mind, where it belonged. Off-limits. Period.

"You're still here?" She bit the words off like she was angry, but he saw the frayed edges of her confidence and her fear hovering underneath the bravado.

"I was expecting more along the lines of *hi, honey, I'm home.*"

She turned on her heel and flopped herself onto the couch. "Pfft."

Achilles watched the curls drift around her head for a moment as she peeled off her jacket and tossed it beside her. *That's it, keep going,* he thought, then mentally slapped himself. He had to stop flirting with her.

He knew he couldn't have her but couldn't seem to stop himself from wanting her. Teasing her tortured him. For centuries, seduction was a sport he had indulged in to pass the time. He'd given his heart once. Now he didn't have one. Flirtation and seduction were the only thing that reminded him that a halfling could create passion in others even if they had no capacity for love themselves.

For whatever reason, this woman, this mortal woman, gave him a phantom ache in his chest where his heart had once beaten centuries ago. Worse, she made him long for things he knew could never be.

And gods help the mentor who was foolish enough to ignore the highest royal edicts binding all vampires. Involvement on an intimate level between mentor and charge was now strictly forbidden for a good reason. Too often the older vampire's powers could become bonded with the fledgling's, forming an imprint neither could resist. Compounding that was a mutual sharing of powers...and pain.

"What did your associate have to say?" He knew, but what the hell, he had to make conversation with her.

Her eyes flashed fire. "I don't want to talk about it."

Yeah, he bet. No more than he wanted to think about what could happen if he were stupid enough to let an imprint form.

Breaking that imprint, or losing it, was an incredibly painful process he never planned to repeat. The fledgling could die a painful death during the transition, or worse. And he'd lived with worse for as long as he could re-member.

For him, his mentor's capture and eventual agonizing death, had been worse than death. Beheading him would have been merciful and put him out of centuries of living in an emotional wasteland as a halfling.

The seven weeks Ione had been tortured during the Spanish Inquisition were still a fresh and agonizing memory over five hundred years later. Every slash of the whip on her pale flesh had cut into Achilles's flesh as well, but without a mark—only the pain. The ripping apart of her tendons and muscles on the rack each day, since they grew anew each night, had left him unable to walk or move. Each time they applied the burning pokers to her supple body, he could taste the smoke of burning flesh and feel the searing heat. And when she'd been beheaded, he'd been struck blind, mute and deaf for a week, waking a halfling, unable to hope, unable to find joy, unable to love.

The memories caused a film of moisture to collect on his skin. He didn't have the need to sweat. No vampire did. But that didn't mean that under times of extreme duress he didn't do so out of pure gut-wrenching terror.

He'd experienced Ione's pain as they'd tortured her, and it had been so physically intense he'd been curled up like a newborn babe.

At the time, when he was the fledgling, he hadn't realized how intense and binding the mentor-fledgling imprint could be. But now, from bitter experience, he knew.

And he never, *ever,* wanted to feel that helpless again, especially with someone he couldn't trust.

Nor did he want to place that burden on anyone else—especially Rebecca.

"Something tells me it wasn't what you expected."

She glanced at him, her eyes softening just a touch. Pain tainted the air with the acidic tang of vinegar.

He needed to keep things light and easy between them. No interest, no attraction. Purely platonic. He had to treat her, *see* her, as his little sister until he determined her true loyalties. He forced a lighthearted grin as he looked at her. "Tough day at the office, sweetling?"

"Those jerks suspended my contract. They kicked me off my own damn project! And apparently, for the moment, I'm becoming a vampire."

"That calls for a drink." Gods knew he needed one. The moment her scent had hit him, his fangs had tried to engage. Achilles pressed his tongue against the barely protruding tips, forcing them back inside.

He reached up and materialized a glass with ice. From the thin air, a stream of pale amber liquid began to fill it and he offered it to her. "An amaretto sour for the lady."

Beck didn't have time to be astonished because the rampant curiosity that had pushed her into becoming a scientist overrode any fears. "How did you do that?" She reached for the glass, inspected it and took a sip. It was perfect. "And how did you know what I like?"

He had the temerity to grin at her as if it were his own special little secret.

All it did was bump up her determination another notch. "You should confess and tell me. I'm becoming a vampire, even if it's temporarily, so you might as well let me in on how all this works because I'll figure it out eventually."

"Just so you can use it for your research?"

She shrugged. "Perhaps."

"Has Kristin never phased or materialized items in front of you?"

"Ah, no."

Achilles phased himself a cold bottle of beer, small beads of condensation streaking down the bottle, and took a long draw. "It just isn't the same."

"What?"

He held up the bottle. "Beer. Gods, I miss good Egyptian beer made with honey."

"I'm sorry, what does that have to do with phasing or materializing or whatever it is you call it?"

"You can bring items to you, but you can't replicate them."

"What do you mean?"

"I mean I can't bring back my stallion from Greece. Gods, he was magnificent. I can't phase myself an Egyptian beer that was brewed in the old ways two millennia ago. I can't bring back those who've died." His voice cracked and he cleared his throat. For a moment he seemed too far away, his green eyes glassy rather than filled with the sparkling intensity she'd come to expect. He closed his eyes, let out a long slow breath and tipped up his beer bottle, draining it in one continuous swallow.

When he opened his eyes he seemed more himself

again, and flicked his gaze in her direction. "I'm limited to calling to me what is here, what exists in this time. Even vampires have to live in the here and now. Which is no problem when you're young." He gave her a wink that made her stomach flip. "But as you age, it gets to be rather tedious. One misses things."

"But how does it work?"

He gave her a knowing smile that shimmied up her spine in a head-to-toe burst of tingling electricity and made her aware of how odd it was to have a man, a big man, so relaxed in her home. As much as he seemed out of place in her decidedly feminine living room, he also seemed perfectly at home, as if he belonged there. Which made her all the more wary.

She knew she was the kind of person who'd fallen in lust at first sight a time or two. But that wasn't exactly what she wanted any more. She didn't want love, exactly. Love hurt. Growing up as the illegitimate child of a powerful man meant she was neither to be seen nor heard. And when her mom left one benefactor and moved on to the next, everyone and everything she'd come to rely on disappeared, giving her a photo box of fading memories, no roots and one or two good friends—but no one who truly knew her. And, once her mother had hooked up with Victor, who had money and power, she never saw or heard from her again. Oh, it had taken her awhile to figure out who and what he was. But by then all contact with her mother was long gone. She wasn't going to repeat her mother's life by relying on a man, or a vampire, for anything.

Sexy as hell or not, she wanted more than a few months of a mind-numbing fling or years of patronage. She wanted…she wanted to matter.

And mattering to Achilles was as unlikely as her staying a vampire. She was already falling hard in lust with the hunk sprawled out in her recliner. With a guy who treated her like a kid sister. Or worse—a job.

"Why don't you come sit with me and I can explain it to you."

Where? In your lap? Fat chance, she thought, eyeing the recliner. His words were basic, normal, totally something anyone could have said. Yet the way he said it made all the little hairs on her body sit up and take notice. It was as though he was a sex magnet and she was a sexually charged lodestone.

Damn. She was misinterpreting his signals because she wanted him to be just as attracted to her as she was to him. What had Kris said about vampires having a natural ability to change everything about them into your best fantasy?

"I think it might be better if I just stay over here," she said smoothly, ignoring the skipping beats of her heart as he shot her a lazy whatever-you-want-babe kind of smile. Getting involved with a vampire—especially this vampire—would be a very bad idea.

She was his job, not his potential girlfriend, if vampires even had such things as girlfriends. And in less than two weeks, she hoped, she'd return to her world and he could go back to his. It wasn't a combination for a long-term relationship where either one of them could matter to the other.

He shook his head as if she'd sucked all the fun out of the moment and sighed a harsh breath. The empty bottle vanished into thin air as he sat the recliner in an upward position. "To phase an object, you focus your energy and thought on what you want. You picture its form, its weight, the color, the texture, the scent—anything that makes it real to you and you call it into being in your presence."

Beck's mind started to work on the process, the rules. Every system, biological or otherwise, had rules. If you could figure out the rules, then you could find the missing opportunities—the gaps, and bend the rules to suit your needs. It was the basis of genetic engineering. "But it has to already exist somewhere else to get it to you."

"Yes."

"Well, you told me how it works, but not the actual process behind it. Are you shifting molecules, using wormholes, extrapolating energy signatures, creating a particle by particle anomaly in quantum space like a wireless facsimile machine that pops out actual objects rather than just duplicated images?"

He simply stared at her as if she'd spoken pure gibberish.

"You don't have a clue what I'm saying do you?"

His green gaze grew sharper, more penetrating so that she suddenly had the odd impression that he was poking around the recesses of her mind. "You have a hard time simply accepting anything, don't you?"

Beck squirmed. Knowing the why and how made accepting things easier. Especially the things a person didn't want to accept. Things like cruelty, abandonment, death, disease, fear, anxiety and loss. If one could just understand the how and the why, they all became easier to bear somehow.

His brow furrowed slightly as he brushed his hand through his hair. "The truth is I've never asked the kinds of questions you do. It was enough to survive and thrive and learn how to navigate the new life that was given to me. If you want more exacting answers, you'll have to ask the clan's medical and scientific personnel."

Her eyes went wide. "You have labs?"

The sparkle of intelligence and excitement in her hazel eyes widened the band of green around her dark pupils and made his fangs throb. Her request was unusual, but then everything about her was. That was part of what made her so utterly tempting and made him forget to be wary. He had to stop thinking of her that way. Achilles doubled his determination to look at her as just another fledgling.

"Oh, there's labs aplenty and gadgets enough to keep you interested, I'm certain. I'll see what I can do to get you an introduction to some of our top medical and scientific people and you can ask all those burning questions I can hear spinning around in that head of yours."

"That would be great. Really great. Thank you," she said in a quiet voice as she turned on her heel.

Her face might be soft and pliant, but her eyes were focused and a million miles away. Achilles knew her well enough by now to know that her brain was fizzling and popping with possibilities.

He could see by the rapid blinking of her eyes and the steady quick pulse in her throat that she was terrified of what was happening to her. The only way she could combat it was to remain analytical and scientific as her body changed. His admiration for this woman shot up. She was amazingly strong. But she'd need to be, Achilles reminded himself grimly.

He reached into her mind once more and heard the frenzied one-sided conversation she held with herself. *If they have an electron microscope, I could continue my research. There would be access to more ichor. Hey, what if I could get Margo to come here? We might be able to truly finish the vaccine. Then Kristin and I and so many others could be free. I wouldn't have to be a vampire. Mom wouldn't have to—*

Her thoughts snapped him back from his musings to reality. Dmitri was right. She had no intention of giving up her plans to create the vaccine, despite being cast aside by the investors. As long as she was bent on creating a weapon of mass destruction to his kind, she was still the enemy, a vulnerable enemy, but one not to be trusted.

Chapter 5

Across the girly living room, with its floral furniture and cutesy knickknacks, Rebecca hardly looked like a threat. But behind that heart-shaped face and sweet lips lay a mind far more brilliant than Machiavelli.

Why the hell was creating the vaccine so damned important to her? It was a quest. A Holy Grail. Why did it matter so much? That's what he needed to find out.

Achilles said nothing more and let her leave the room. Her head swarmed with thoughts he no longer felt like hearing. Let her plot and plan all she wanted. The transition had already begun, and no amount of scientific hoodoo was going to stop it. He could already smell the faint change in her blood, the spicy scent of it growing more complex with vampire pheromones.

As much discomfort and confusion as she caused him,

he dared not leave her. There was no telling how long her transition would take. She would need to feed soon and he had serious doubts she'd be willing to look for a donor. He had to stay to feed her. He'd come into being a vampire willingly. Rebecca hadn't. Big difference.

Of course, his own choices had repercussions. *He'd* fallen for *his* mentor before the transition had even started. He hadn't been aware of the consequences, and even if he had, he'd been too raw, too full of male need to care.

Ione could have been a goddess in her own right. When he'd seen her at the temple of the bull-god Vrishabha over two and a half millennia ago, he'd been stunned by her ethereal beauty. For days he could neither sleep nor eat. She'd captivated him. So he'd approached her.

"Why have you come to this temple? Do you wish to be a warrior among warriors, Spartan?" The silvery quality of her voice sounded like chimes in the wind.

He looked at her fiercely, putting all the emotion he had been strictly trained throughout his life not to voice into his eyes. "I do." Almost as much as I want you.

She'd looked deeply in his eyes, her delicate fingers stroking his face in a way that burned through him. She'd taken him to her chambers, the night burned into his memory like none other. And for the first time, he believed in love. Not just the power of a woman's body to ease his own, but in a need far deeper than hunger or thirst. In her arms he'd found completion, and something a warrior never expected he'd want—peace.

So when she took him by the hand in the nights that

followed, he went willingly, spending each night with her and leaving her bed at dawn. Until the last night. The night when she had changed him.

Her eyes glowed like a blue flame, a smile curving her lips. "I would like to give you a gift. You will be stronger than a hundred of your finest men. Able to go without food or water and fight with the speed of the wind. Your enemies will fall down before you. Would you accept this gift from me, and Vrishabha?"

Achilles would have vaulted the waters that separated Greece from Crete had she asked it. "I would."

As a priestess for the bull-god Vrishabha, Ione seemed larger than life to him, her dark hair flowing over the flawless alabaster skin of her bared shoulders. She'd turned back to the horned altar, her hair a dark river cascading down to her waist. The light from the golden braziers illuminated the fine linen of her robes, rendering them translucent. His breath had caught at the wonder of her body, and the full sexual rush she stirred in him that was more important than the call of battle, more intense than the thrill of a victory over his enemies. Things he had been taught to cherish above all else.

She turned, her profile glowing in the firelight, her blue eyes so intense they seemed violet. In her hands she held a golden chalice engraved with images of the ancient gods, and studded with egg-sized dark bloodred rubies. At her wrist a cut marred her perfect skin, a thin black liquid oozing from it. "Do you willingly sacrifice yourself to the service of Vrishabha?"

*His heart swelled, beating hard against his sternum.
Ready. Willing. Excited. "I do."*

"Then kneel, Spartan."

*Achilles sank to his knees on the cold marble floor.
Gazing up into her exquisite face, his heart overflowed
with so much love he couldn't contain it. He wanted to
feel this way for eternity. Beyond eternity. He'd never
in his life felt this much emotion, this much love. The
sheer rightness of their love filled him to the brim.*

*Eyes glowing, Ione extended the goblet. "Drink from
Vrishabha's chalice, my Achilles."*

*He took it from her pale slender hands. The metal
felt cool between his palms, emitting a faint vibration
that traveled up his forearms. The dark surface of the
liquid reflected his own face, alive and alert and eager
for what his ladylove promised.*

*Achilles lifted it to his mouth, drinking greedily of
the dark liquid, a wine laced with something he couldn't
identify. Ignoring the slightly dark sweet aftertaste, his
gaze never left her beautiful face.*

*Within mere minutes the hunger had taken over,
eating at him like a slow drip of acid spreading through
his bloodstream until every cell of his body cried out for
sustenance.*

*And Ione had brought it to him. A maiden in training
for the temple of Vrishabha—the original donors who
eagerly participated in a rite that brought them pleasure
and gave vampires strength.*

Achilles seriously doubted that Rebecca would be
so willing to feed. In fact he'd bet his beloved Bugatti

Veyron that she'd balk at feeding from a live donor of any kind no matter how the hunger ate at her.

She was a scientist. Therefore reason was her drug of choice. In that spirit, he'd prepared several quarts of bagged blood for her to drink.

In any battle the trick was to understand your enemy. While he didn't totally regard Rebecca as his enemy, neither could he trust her. Her rational reasoning nature reminded him of those damned Athenians. People who believed that intellect, inquest and discussion could cure all problems. If there was a second thing he'd learned in centuries on this earth it was that sometimes life was just messy.

A shriek erupted from the vicinity of Rebecca's kitchen. Achilles phased beside a hysterical Rebecca instantly. He placed his hands on her small shoulders. Mistake.

She whipped around as if his touch burned and punched at his chest. "What the *hell* is that?"

"What?"

"That, that stuff in *my* fridge!" She pointed an accusing finger at the interior of her refrigerator.

"Dinner."

"Oh, no, no, no, no. No and hell, no." She gave a full body shiver. "That's blood."

Achilles closed his eyes and pinched the bridge of his nose praying to Vrishabha for patience in guiding this young one.

"You're going to have to feed, Rebecca. I thought this might be easier for you than finding a live donor."

She skewered him with a hard glare, the brown pulsing in her eyes as if she had an internal bullshit meter. "I'm not hungry." Her stomach rumbled in protest loud enough for the neighbors to hear.

Achilles quirked a brow and folded his arms over his chest. "You're not going to die on my watch, fledgling. You *will* eat."

Rebecca gave a nervous glance at the plastic packets all filled with sluggish red liquid. Her skin grew cold and clammy all over and the base of her throat seemed to swell. She shook her head and glanced at the large man beside her who was clearly unaffected by the sight of so much blood.

"You don't understand. Blood makes me—" She bolted from the room and made it to the bathroom down the hall just in time. She bent at the waist and gripped the porcelain, dry heaves undulated along her whole body. God, how embarrassing was this?

Achilles blocked the doorway, watching her. "Go away," she managed to mutter. "Can't you give a girl some space?"

"So blood upsets you?"

Rebecca threw him a nasty glare. "I told you I'm not cut out to be a vampire." Pain, very real pain followed by a searing heat speared up through her stomach into her esophagus causing her to gasp and fall to her knees.

Without a word Achilles gently scooped her up into his arms and carried her to her bed. She was shaking. Logically this made no sense. But she supposed becoming a vampire wasn't anything she'd actually studied before. She knew the virus was continuing to colonize her body. What she didn't understand was how on earth drinking blood could possibly make this any better. It wouldn't stop the virus. It wouldn't protect her system from further invasion.

"This stinks," she groaned as she doubled up around the pain. "Don't you people have vampire Midol or something for this?"

Achilles actually blushed. "Vampires don't…that is we have no need… I'll be right back." He spun on his heel and came back with a glass in hand filled with what looked an awful lot like a Bloody Mary complete with a stalk of celery.

"I tried to cut it for you into something more palatable. Despite how you feel, I can tell you this is the only remedy. The pain will only get worse until you feed."

Beck eyed the glass in his hand as if he were handing her nasty cough syrup rather than a drink. "All I want to know is does that have vodka in it?" If she had to drink bl—no, she couldn't even think about it before the nausea came back with a vengeance—perhaps she could be drunk enough she wouldn't care what was in the mix.

He gave her a broad fangless smile. "What do you think?"

She took the proffered glass with a shaking hand and took a sample whiff. Tomato, lime, celery, a weird metallic scent she didn't want to think about too much. She tried to hand the glass back to him. "I don't think I can do this." God, she didn't want to do this. Never had wanted to do this. It somehow violated the laws of nature.

"It might help if you pinch your nose while drinking."

Beck sighed, then pinched her nose and lifted the glass to her lips. The taste was tangy, and unexpectedly a bit sweet. *Don't think about it. Just keep drinking.* She banged down the empty glass on her beside table as if it'd been a shot rather than a full eight ounces of who knew what. "There. Finished it."

The edge of his sculpted mouth tilted up at the corner with amusement. "And how do you feel?"

She took inventory of her body. The shaking had stopped. Maybe it had just been low blood sugar, she thought, but that didn't explain the odd tingling sensation that was spreading through her system. She pushed herself off the bed and stood.

Suddenly her vision seemed to shift, as if someone had shoved an electron microscope in front of her. She could see the individual threads in Achilles's sweater, even pick out the pattern of how the thread was spiraled together like an unending double helix of DNA. She shifted her gaze upward and was struck by the fringe of dark lashes, each one spiked and thick and somehow got lost in a sea of green. Beck blinked and everything went back to looking normal.

Her joints had become loose and pliable and she felt the floor suddenly shift beneath her feet before being caught in Achilles's strong arms and pressed tightly up against his firm muscular chest and six-pack abs.

"You still have a pulse," he said, shock flickering in his eyes for a moment. His throat moved as he swallowed.

"I take it that's not normal after a first feeding?"

"It should have stopped by now."

"Maybe my cells are just as stubborn as I am."

"I wouldn't be surprised. But the weakness is normal. Wait until your body absorbs a bit more. The first time the rush in the system can be a bit overpowering."

"This is worse than a college bender." Beck wasn't absolutely sure that the sensations flooding her system, particularly the throbbing between her thighs, could be attributed to whatever blood rush he was talking about.

In fact, given the shivers racing along her veins as he set her back on her unsteady feet, she was pretty certain they had to do more with the sex god holding her. She stared at him and inhaled sharply when his eyes met hers, and matched the stare.

Rosemary and mint mingled in the air around him, strong and earthy, clean and seductive, totally, utterly masculine.

Beck noticed the small twin points of polished white peeping out from beneath his sculpted upper lip and gasped. "Um, your fangs are showing."

Achilles smiled, revealing his matched set in all their pearly glory. "Perhaps you'd better check your own."

She tentatively ran the tip of her tongue along the rounded edge of her upper lip and ran into two unfamiliar points.

She stared up at him, her eyes wide. "Oh, my God. Oh. My. God. I have fangs!"

"First blood usually brings them out."

Her fingers streaked up to touch them, and Achilles caught her hand in his, a snap of electricity arcing between them that zapped straight from his hand to his heart. "Careful. They're sharp."

She glanced down at their joined hands. "Is it normal for my senses to be this heightened?"

"Being vampire isn't just about diet. You're a completely different kind of being."

Her eyes narrowed. "And what about what's happening between us. Is that just a vampire thing, too?"

For a moment Achilles was struck dumb. How could he possibly explain how in one kiss he'd already marked her as his own? How could he explain that his own experience was the reason why he'd never touch her either, no matter how much he desired her?

"The mentor-fledgling relationship is unique. It only happens when a vampire is unable to be led through the transition by his or her maker."

"Oh." She said it so softly that it was a mere breath. "So that makes me some kind of vampire orphan or something?"

He cracked a smile for her benefit. "Someone donated the ichor that created your vaccine. We don't know who, but we're working on it. For now, you're my responsibility." And his own personal torment, he added silently. But that was hardly her fault.

"And what happens when we find out?"

Making sure she was steady on her feet, he pulled away from her placing as much distance between them as he could. "That's up to you."

Chapter 6

"Are you feeling well enough to venture out?" Achilles crossed his arms, locking them firmly in place so he wasn't tempted to touch the silken softness of her skin. The afternoon had passed quickly—outside darkness gathered.

Beck shrugged and swiped at the long spiral of hair from her face, shoving her fingers through her wayward curls. A look of disgust scrunched up her small nose, making the scatter of freckles all but disappear. "Oh, for the love of— I've got thicker hair, seriously?" she huffed. "What else is this transition process supposed to do besides mess with my eating habits and change my hair to beyond unmanageable?"

You mean besides making you totally irresistible and totally unattainable to every male vampire in a 500-mile radius? "The easiest way for me to show you would be to take you where other vampires gather so you can see for yourself."

"You mean like a field trip, professor?"

He nodded. "But we need a few rules to keep you safe. First, listen to your mentor, it could save your life."

She crossed her arms, which pressed her breasts closer together. Achilles forced himself to look away from her chest and focus on the rebellious curiosity in her eyes instead.

"Aren't I becoming undead? Kind of hard to hurt the undead."

"Medically speaking. But what is undeath, but another form of life?"

She rolled her eyes. "You're not going to go all metaphysical on me, are you? I prefer to stick to the facts."

"Fact. We are undead rather than truly immortal."

She waved a hand as if swiping at a particular annoying fly. "Undead. Immortal. Same petri dish. You can't die."

"Don't be fooled, sweetling. Vampires can still be harmed, even killed in the right circumstances." An image of Ione curled in agony speared through his mind, a phantom pain searing through him like a red-hot knife.

"Pfft. Yeah, like a stake the size of a California redwood?"

He clenched his hand into a fist and banished the image and the pain. He focused on the sprinkle of brown across the green background of her eyes, the way the freckles danced across the bridge of her nose. Focused on the woman before him here and now.

"Stakes, garlic, holy water are all fabrications. Beheading is the only true method to kill a vampire. Silver and dead man's blood are also harmful and painful but not enough to end our existence."

Her jaw slackened. "You're kidding me, right?"

"No. Listen closely. I'm teaching you. Rule two, not all vampires are nice. So watch yourself."

"So where are we going for our field trip?"

"Sangria."

"You mean that freaky vampire club downtown?"

He smiled. "You've been there?"

"Only once to meet Kristin."

A slight buzzing started in the back of her head followed by an echoing voice that wasn't her own. More disturbingly it was his. *Is that where you obtained the ichor for your vaccine?*

She glared at him, backing up a pace and covering her ears with her hands. "What the hell? Are you in my head?"

He grinned. *Rule three. Guard your thoughts. Vampires can talk to each other via mental communication. The closer the link to the vampire, the easier the communication.*

Her eyes widened. "Can I do that, too?"

He nodded.

She concentrated with all her might. *Then stay out of my head!*

His sculpted lips flattened into a firm line. "You may

find it helpful at some point if you need to reach me and we are not within eye contact."

Had he actually heard her? "Why can't you people use cell phones like the rest of us?" she muttered under her breath so he couldn't hear.

"It's cheaper," he answered, tapping his ear. "Rule four. Watch what you say. Don't think you can whisper in the club and get away with it. Along with your heightened sense of smell and sight, you'll also be able to hear far more than you did before. So can all the vampires around you. Only they've had more time to refine and control their abilities."

"Anything else?"

"I'll drive."

Grabbing her navy wool peacoat and her purse, she followed him out of her front door into the night.

On the cracked concrete of her driveway sat a sleek, low-slung black sports car with big fenders and a stubbed back end like a Corvette that seemed to hug the ground. There was only one way to truly describe it—fast looking. She'd never seen anything like it, which suited him.

She whistled long and low. "I've never seen a car like that before. What is it?"

"Bugatti Veyron. Sang Noir edition."

"Never heard of it." She peered closer. Achilles opened the door for her.

"Red? They gave it a bloodred interior?"

"I believe they call it crimson and it was a special order. It came standard with a tangerine interior I wasn't sure I could stomach." He shut her door and quickly climbed in behind the wheel. Everything inside spoke of luxurious excess. The buttery soft leather seats cradled her body, the space-shuttle version of a dashboard made her eyes widen and the exquisite new car smell tickled her senses.

She glanced at him as he revved up the engine. "I thought you liked your horse from Greece."

He slowly grazed his fingers over the curve of the leather wrapped steering wheel in obvious appreciation. "This little baby has 1200 horses under the hood. And it's much, much faster. I miss my horse. But I don't think I'd trade. My horse in Greece didn't cost two point seven mill."

He pressed the pedal down and the engine growled. Beck's pulse kicked up a notch in anticipation. She'd always had a secret passion for fast things.

"How fast?"

"You mean how fast will it go?"

She nodded.

He peered at her intensely. "You like fast things, don't you?"

She just looked at him. "I'm not going to dignify that with a response."

The car jumped away from the curb as he whipped a 180-degree turn into traffic, tires squealing. Beck grabbed the handle on the passenger door and grinned like a kid on a carnival ride.

"It'll go over 250 miles an hour. But you run out of gas in about twelve minutes at that speed."

"Is that just a fact hidden in your brain or did you actually test it for yourself?"

He gave her a wicked grin. "Why take some scientist's word, when you can test it out yourself?"

Everything outside the car rushed by in a blur, the city lights streaming together. She pinched her lips together fighting off the wave of anger that washed over her at her situation and at herself. As much as she fantasized about doing exciting things, the time or two she'd tried something out of her comfort zone it had backfired drastically, particularly when it involved people she cared about.

She closed her eyes and a flash of her mom's face filled her vision. She'd gone off to college, a fourteen-year-old freshman super brain and when she'd come home at winter break it was to find her mom had taken up with her new gentleman friend. The moment she had met him, she knew there was something strange about him. She'd just shaken it off, telling herself he was that way because he was rich and eccentric. She should have trusted her gut and known her mother was in trouble. But Mom always had to find out things for herself. She'd been so angry when Beck broached the subject.

"Self-testing isn't always something I'd recommend," Beck said, her voice far less confident than she planned.

"True. But then how would you ever know what you were really missing?"

She stared hard at his profile. The night cut it to a fine edge, his nose straight, his cheekbones hard-edged. He wasn't the type to back off from a battle, verbal or not. "You aren't talking about cars anymore."

"Neither are you."

He could teach her everything he wanted to, but it didn't mean she still wasn't going to use every moment to her advantage. Despite her newfound abilities, she still didn't want to be a vampire anymore than she wanted her mother or her best friend to be one. The sooner she found a way to reverse the process the better. Then she could go back to a life she understood. One with rules and absolutes, not the confused craziness she'd entered since she started dabbling in manipulating the vampire virus.

He pulled up the car to the curb outside the club. Throbbing red neon pulsed the name Sangria in swooping cursive letters over the padded leather door. Beck sighed, gnawing at her lip.

"You aren't scared to go in, are you?" Achilles nudged. "I'll be with you the entire time."

She glanced at him. "It isn't the company that scares me."

"What is it then?"

Her eyes strayed back to the padded leather door. How could she tell him that it was the fear that she'd stay this way. What if she couldn't find a cure? What if she had to accept that this was going to be her new life? Surely Margo had seen some sort of results with the PCR method by now. She'd have to call her since it was clear Margo wasn't going to get back in touch.

She twisted in her seat, putting her back to the club outside. "I want to understand how all this works."

"You mean being a vampire?"

"No, how you all became vampires in the first place. The virus had to originate somewhere."

He hooked his wrist over the steering wheel and looked deeply into her eyes, impatience shimmering in the air around him. "If I give you the Cliff Notes version, will you go inside?"

She glanced at the door and shivered. Crossing that threshold meant something totally different to her now than it had eight months ago. Then she'd been completely floored, like the rest of the world, to discover that vampires were even real. She'd been determined to protect humans from them. Now she was becoming one herself. "Yeah. I guess."

"Thousands of years ago, a man name Siphidius impressed the gods and they offered him eternal life. He took them up on the offer, not realizing that the bull-god Vrishabha, in whose image he'd been recreated, demanded blood sacrifices. The fangs we have are just the horns of the Mesopotamian bull god in another form. And the draught they gave Siphidius was vampire venom."

"Was the virus in that venom?"

"No. Centuries later, when Siphidius nearly became ruler of the known world and thought that he too should be a god, the gods thought he needed a smack down. So he got his ass handed to him in the form of a virus. It's been passed down genetically to every vampire since then. Some survive it but most succumb every thousand years when the virus turns vicious, reverting them to their true chronological age in forty-eight hours. It's only been in the last changing that the nasty side effect of the virus was stopped cold."

"Did you create an antiviral?"

"No. Nature did. She's called Evaline St. Croix and she's the one who stopped the virus from wiping out yet another generation."

Beck's curiosity spiked. "Any chance I could get to meet her?"

One corner of Achilles's mouth lifted in a cocky self-assured half smile. "I think I can arrange it. Is that enough to get you in the door, or do you need me to explain how vampires are traditionally made, too?"

Beck shook her head. If she could get a shot at meeting this wonder vamp who'd shut down the virus, then she wanted to get to it as soon as possible. "No, I'm good. Let's go meet some vampires."

He exited the car and opened her door for her. Getting out of a car so low down to the ground was harder than she expected and she glanced around for something she could grab to propel herself out of the seat.

He held out a smooth, blunt-fingered hand to her. Beck took it. An electric arc zinged up from her fingertips to her mouth, making her heart beat hard and fast. She gasped at the sensation. A quick glance at the glint in his eyes confirmed she wasn't the only one who'd felt the connection between them.

"A hazard of the mentor-fledgling relationship. Everything is felt more intensely because of the bond."

She nodded and bit her lip. More intense? Good grief. The last thing she needed was for anything to be more intense around Achilles. He already had her on edge with the sexual allure that radiated off him like a heat signature. "Who are we meeting?"

"Kristin and Dmitri."

Beck wanted to squee with giddy delight. She hadn't seen her best friend in weeks because of their messed up day-night schedules now that Kris was a vampire. "What are you waiting for?" she asked shoving open the door of the club, leaving Achilles to catch up.

She'd only been here once before, because honestly once had been enough. The interior of Sangria looked like a spelunker's dream hangout. Up-lit stalactites dripped down from the ceiling while down-lit stalagmites jutted up from the floor. Honestly, they all looked like giant stone fangs to her. The only thing that made this place even qualify as an upscale trendy bar were the modern black-and-chrome fixtures, the shiny black lacquered bar lit from beneath with red neon and the big mahogany dance floor sporting some kind of weird symbol made from three intertwined circles.

A row of crimson curtains covered the doorways leading to the private rooms off the side of the dance floor. She'd been in the farthest one when Kris had given her vampire ichor to use in her testing.

Beck let her gaze trail over the booths decked out in plush crimson velvet, looking for Kris's familiar face and long blond hair among the people packed into the club and moving around like test tubes in a centrifuge.

Achilles lightly touched her elbow with the tips of his fingers, but she felt the contact like the brush of a flame against her skin. "Can I get you a drink?"

"No. I'm good. I'm just going to head over to see Kris if that's all right with you."

Achilles made eye contact with Kris across the room and Beck could tell there was some kind of conversation mind-thingy going on between the two of them just by the look of concentration on his face.

"She said Dmitri's in his office. I'll go speak with him while you visit with her."

Beck bounced up to the balls of her feet. "Perfect. See you back here in about an hour, professor?"

"Don't get into any trouble."

"Me? Never."

A corner of his mouth tipped up making his lips look far too kissable. "Somehow I seriously doubt that. If you get hungry, sweetling, don't be afraid to call for me," he said as he brushed the tip of his index finger over the end of her nose.

A man like that could make a woman hungry just by saying hello. Beck gave herself a shake. Kris. She was going to walk over and see Kris. Yeah. That was the plan.

"Bye." She wiggled her fingers and turned on her heel before she did anything incredibly stupid like kissing him. Beck squeezed and twisted through the moving crowd at the edge of the dance floor.

A solid chest decked out in a black T-shirt, slashed faded blue jeans and long black leather duster blocked her path. She was forced to look upward at the huge guy who'd deliberately blocked her way. A pair of shocking red eyes stared down at her. He had to be a vampire. His platinum hair stood up in hedgehog fashion, spiky and stiff, making him look a lot like an early cover shot of rocker Billy Idol. Two words came to mind just looking at him: bad news. A shiver crawled up her spine and Beck stepped back a pace.

"Excuse me," she said, her words laced with a heavy dose of asperity.

He placed a hefty hand covered in a black spiked fingerless leather glove on her shoulder. "Have we met before?"

Beck glanced at his hand, then leveled her best back-off glare at him. "I'd think I'd remember. And it doesn't ring a bell. If you'll just—"

He closed his eyes for a brief second, inhaling deeply and when he opened his eyes they turned from bright red to dark crimson, nearly the color of blood. "You smell just like Stacy." Beck's stomach started to swim and swish uncomfortably. Her mother's name was Stacy. This guy was completely creeping her out. She glanced over her shoulder to see if Achilles was anywhere in sight. He wasn't.

"You're a fledgling, aren't you?"

Beck let out a long-suffering sigh. "Look, my friend is over there waiting for me. Nice chatting with you."

"My name is Vane." He looked deeply in her eyes like he expected her to remember it.

"Vane. That's…different. Well, Vane, I'm here with someone and I don't think he'd really appreciate you hitting on me."

He nodded, his lip curling in nearly a smile. "I know. He's a fool to leave you alone." He paused, his eyes changing, flashing to dark brown for an instant. "You really don't remember me, do you?"

Beck gasped. With the change in eye color his face seemed more familiar. But Victor, her mother's vampire gentleman friend, had dark hair, not platinum blond.

"Ah, I see some spark of recognition."

Beck's legs wobbled. It was not possible. This had to be somebody's sick vampire initiation joke.

"You're too tempting for any full-blooded vampire to resist. I'm sure we'll meet again."

Beck couldn't get away from him quickly enough. As fast as she could, she side-stepped him and moved toward Kris who had left the booth and was striding purposely toward her. Just a few steps more and she could collapse.

Kris reached out and Beck pulled her into a bear hug. "God, it's good to see you," Beck said.

Kris gazed out into the crowd, her blue eyes wary. "Was that vampire bothering you?"

Beck waved her hand in the air in a gesture of dismissal, trying not to think about what Victor had done to her mother, and refusing to think that Victor might be parading about as Vane. "Nothing to worry about. Just

some vampire with freaky red eyes trying to hit on me."
She glanced over her shoulder again and couldn't find a
trace of the platinum spiked hair anywhere, which was
odd considering that guy had to be a full head taller than
most of the people in the club.

"He didn't happen to give you his name did he?" Kris
asked.

"Yeah. Vane. How weird is that?"

Kris visibly blanched and swayed, which only rein-
forced her own fears more.

"What? Kris, are you okay?"

"What the hell does he want with you?" The shake
in Kris's voice alarmed her even more.

Beck shrugged and shook her head. "Got me. I just
literally ran into him. Jerk wouldn't move out of my way
or take a hint to get lost. He tried to pretend he knew
me."

Kris grabbed a hold of her in a no-nonsense grip, her
brows bent in a deep V over stormy blue eyes. "Listen
to me, Beck. That was a seriously badass vampire you
don't want to be involved with. He's dangerous."

Kris's over-the-top reaction to the vampire was
giving Beck a serious case of the heebie-jeebies and
small shivers of fear scurried over her skin making
gooseflesh in their wake. "No worries. We didn't exactly
hit it off."

"What did he say to you?"

"Asked if we'd met before." Beck gave a brittle laugh
trying to ease the tension stifling the air between her and
her best friend. "Jeez, you would think that vampires

could come up with a better pick up line." She didn't like feeling as if she'd just committed a major faux pas without knowing what she'd done wrong. But something was definitely wrong.

"Did you notice anything unusual?" Kris pushed.

"It wasn't like I was looking at him so much as trying to get around him," Beck hedged. "The only thing I thought was really weird was that his eyes shifted color from bright red to dark crimson—and he said I smelled like Stacy." Her voice broke.

Kris grabbed her by the hand and started plowing straight through the crowd. "We need to see Dmitri, *now*."

Chapter 7

"Vane was in Sangria? Why the hell didn't anybody catch him?" Dmitri smacked his wide desk with the rounded side of his fist, putting a hole straight through the three-inch-thick mahogany top.

The nicely appointed manager's office seemed small with the two large men already taking up more than half of it. Kris stood beside Beck, arms crossed, concern creasing downward lines around her pinched lips. Achilles stood beside Dmitri, the guys on one side of the desk and the girls on the other.

Beck glanced around nervously. Where exactly was the nearest exit? The walls were covered in something that looked vaguely like red leather and the same black lacquer and chrome motif that decorated thc club extended into Dmitri's personal space. No windows. Only one door in and one door out.

"Easy," Achilles said mildly as he brushed the fine coating of wood dust from his dark leather jacket. Man, did Dmitri have a short fuse.

"Hey, it's not like anything happened." *Much.* "He just hit on me by trying to pretend he knew me."

Achilles ground his teeth together making his jaw pop. He moved toward her. "I never should have left you alone."

Annoyance bubbled up inside of her. "Nothing. Happened."

His gaze bored into her, green and intense. "I— *We're* worried. He's tracking your scent."

"What?"

He pointed at his own green eyes, which suddenly shifted to palest gray and back again, and startled her enough to make her heart skip a beat. "The change in his eye color. He's tracking your scent. For whatever reason you set him off."

"But I didn't *do* anything!" Beck protested.

Achilles looked directly at her, suddenly seeming far older and weary. "You didn't have to." He turned and spread his hands wide on what was left of Dmitri's desk. "We need to find out what he wants."

Dmitri's gaze shifted to his wife, Kristin, and then to Beck who stood beside her. Beck shivered. She hadn't seen it earlier, but Dmitri was just as worried as he was angry. He narrowed his eyes at his friend. "Whatever he wants, he thinks he can use your new fledgling to obtain it."

Achilles growled.

Dmitri looked her up and down and Beck felt the overwhelming urge to squirm as if she were a specimen under a microscope. "There's got to be some connection between the two of them."

Achilles stepped closer, heat radiating off of him to wrap around her. "You mean one that has nothing to do with your traitorous blood brother playing yet another game with you?"

Dmitri growled back. "It's not like I invited him here. He knows this is clan territory."

"And since when has a reiver given a damn about who owns what? They take what they like, when they like and kill whoever gets in their way. Well, blood brother or not, if he comes near Rebecca again, I'll behead him. I swear it." The veins along Achilles's neck were throbbing. Beck somehow doubted it was a heartbeat, so much as anger pulsing in waves through his black vampire ichor.

Dmitri sat back in his leather chair. "Be my guest."

"Why did he have red eyes?" Beck twisted a bit of her hair around her index finger, something she unconsciously did when she was analyzing, searching for a solution. She glanced down, and realized she was doing it. She felt her cheeks heat and tucked her hand behind her back.

Achilles's pupils dilated slightly. He tore his gaze away from her and focused it on Dmitri. "You want to explain it to her?"

Dmitri stepped around his desk, pacing the length of his office as he spoke. "Vampires have lineages like any other beings. We have makers who function like our mother or father, those who transformed us into vampires. We have *tutores,* mentors, who guide us through the process of learning to become a vampire when our maker cannot. That's the role Achilles is fulfilling for you.

"Every lineage inherits the eye color of their line. In a nest they might all have the same eye color as they change to become more hivelike in their mentality, to the point where the strongest can control the will of them all. Vane is such a vampire. Nesting vampires don't follow the rules of our clan that make it safe for us to live with humans in a symbiotic manner. They live to feed rather than feed to live. That's part of why he's so dangerous."

"So red eyes equals scary bad vampire. Got it," said Beck.

Kris cleared her throat placing her hand on her husband's arm. "Not always. Some of those with red eyes are the oldest lines. Others have had ancient makers. It just happens that Vane, and his maker Larissa, are two vampires with no compunction when it comes to taking human or vampire life. But not every vampire follows the ways of his or her maker." A silent understanding passed between Kristin and Dmitri as he reached to cover her hand with his.

"Vane and Larissa also happen to have very real, very close ties to some of the members of our clan," added

Achilles as he looked directly at Dmitri. "But what I don't get is why Rebecca? We don't even know whose ichor she used in the vaccine."

"Perhaps that's the first place to look," Kris suggested. "My friend Bradley was created by Vane. He ought to have some clue who was running that whole ichor-trading scheme that went down a few months ago."

Beck interrupted. "He said I smelled like Stacy. Now I don't know if he was just doing it to creep me out, or because he knows something about my mom. But for a second, just a second, his eyes turned dark brown."

"A memory before he went rogue," Dmitri muttered. "Might be another connection."

Achilles rubbed his left hand over the tight right fist. "Perhaps I need to pay him a little visit." He glanced at Beck. She'd never seen him this on edge. Whoever or whatever this Vane vampire was, he seemed to really hit all the wrong buttons for Achilles and Dmitri.

He shot Beck a hard look. "Stay with Kris until I can come back for you."

It was an order, not a request, and caused the hair on the back of her neck to bristle. "I can take care of myself."

His gaze flicked to Kris, blatantly ignoring her comment. "Watch her. If she gets hungry, call me." Kris nodded, which bugged Beck. Since when had her best friend turned into her babysitter?

Dmitri and Achilles walked out the office door, closing it behind them without so much as a see-ya-later.

Beck waited a moment or two, just to make sure the guys were gone, then leveled her gaze at her friend. "You're overreacting, Kris. I'm an adult and, shockingly, fairly intelligent. I know this vampire is bad news. I can feel it. I'm not going to do anything stupid. I really don't need a babysitter."

Kris reached over and gave her a shoulder nudge. "Are you saying you don't want to hang with me?"

"No, but—"

"Look, big brain or not, this isn't something to mess with. These boundary disputes between vampires can get pretty messy. He approached you. If Achilles and Dmitri think they need to worry, then there's a reason."

She wasn't used to being hovered over. Watched, yes, but in more of an advisory capacity. Beck always saw herself as taking care of others rather than vice versa. And she preferred it that way.

"We'll just go to my place and hang out," Kristin offered.

"Would you mind if we went back to my house? I think I've dipped my toes deep enough into the vampire pool for one night."

"Sure."

Beck could hear the phone ringing as they neared her front door. Four rings and it would go to voice mail. A niggling sensation in the pit of her stomach told her it was Margo calling. She shoved the key in the lock and turned it. Three rings to go.

Kristin watched her struggling with the lock. "You

want me to answer that? I can phase in and get it for you."

"No. I got it." The door always stuck a little, she pushed her shoulder into it and it popped free, then reached out to flip on a light. Two rings. Beck dashed across the living room, leaving Kris to shut the door behind them, as she spun into the kitchen snagging the phone and glancing at the caller ID. The lab. Margo. She picked up on the last ring.

"I was hoping you'd call. What's the scoop?"

Margo's voice sounded edgy, worried. "I'm glad I caught you. I've already called three times but I didn't want to leave a voice mail on this. I've tried both another cassette method and a PCR substitution but neither are showing results. The vampiriophage is still actively multiplying."

Beck's stomach tightened into an uncomfortable knot. Damn. She'd been really hoping that it was just the method that wasn't perfect, but somehow, considering the reaction she'd seen in Achilles and Dmitri when they'd discussed Vane, she knew that each ichor wasn't created equally. Somehow every vampire's ichor differed, or at least it did in family lines. "Maybe it's the sample we're using."

"What do you mean?" Margo's tone held an edge of skepticism. Beck could hear her clicking and reclicking the end of the pen in her hand. "The vampire ichor?"

"Yeah. I just found out tonight that there's a natural carrier of the antiviral who's alive, well, undead at least.

Her name is Evaline St. Croix. I'm going to try and get a sample of her ichor as soon as I can."

"But aren't they all the same?"

Just a few days ago she'd held much the same opinion of vampires. Now Beck wasn't so sure.

"Apparently not. Regardless, it might be the break we've been looking for to get the vaccine off the ground. I'll call when I have something."

She hung up and felt the heated glare of Kris boring into her back. "You're still working on that damn vaccine?"

Beck twisted, putting her back to the wall. An open chilled bottle of Chardonnay sat on Beck's counter that she knew hadn't been in her refrigerator. Kris looked at her over a glass of wine, her face smooth and unreadable despite the tone of her words. Obviously her friend had settled into being a vampire.

"Want some?"

A bad taste rose up in Beck's mouth. "No, thanks." She shifted her gaze to the bottle and away from Kris's face, finding it difficult to navigate the uncomfortable chasm that had seemed to open like a rift in the earth between her and Kris for the first time in their friendship.

"Not everyone is hunky-dory with being a vampire, Kris. There are a lot of people who never intended to be a vampire, and I thought you were one of them. And there are lots more who are afraid to get a blood transfusion for fear of becoming one. I'm trying to help them regardless of my own deteriorating condition."

Kris sighed. The glass clinked lightly on the counter

as she set it down. Beck glanced up. Kris's face was softer, but pain lurked behind her brilliant blue eyes. She reached forward, placing a consoling hand on Beck's shoulder. "Look, I know you mean well. It's just that this whole vampire society is a lot more complicated that them vs. us. Vampires have a place in this world. We just didn't know it before. And you aren't deteriorating, you're transforming."

"It would've been nice if someone had bothered to *ask* me if I wanted this," Beck said bitterly as she grabbed up Kris's half-finished glass of wine and took a sip. "And what about the people who didn't want it to happen? What about my mom?"

"They should get a choice."

"Exactly." Beck tipped back the glass and polished off the wine in one long swallow. "That's why I'm still working on the vaccine."

"So what are you going to do?"

Beck worried her bottom lip between her teeth as she rubbed the glass between her hands. The implication of what she was trying to accomplish with the vaccine and the precarious balance of life, death and the unrealized aspects of being a vampire hit her full in the gut for the first time. "When?"

"Once you figure this whole vaccine thing out. Are you going back to being human?"

"Absolutely. Aren't you?"

Kris shook her head slowly, her mouth breaking into a warm smile that touched Beck to the heart. "I'm happy for the first time in my life. I've found someone I want to be with for as long as it lasts. And if that means we're both undead, then so be it."

Beck's chest squeezed. What would it be like to matter enough to someone that they'd choose death over life for you? Is that how her mother had felt about Victor? She doubted it. That was more about some messed up need to have someone stronger to cling to than mattering. "Don't you miss being normal?"

"What's 'normal' these days?" Kris shrugged. "You miss aspects of anything when change happens. But that doesn't mean you don't grow to accept and enjoy something new."

"Maybe, but *I...I*—" A sharp pinching sensation clamped down inside Beck's gut and she doubled up around the pain, the glass falling from her hand before she could stop it.

Kris was by her side in an instant, arm around her. "What's wrong?"

Beck's midsection audibly gurgled. "Either I'm about to run to the bathroom, or the Bloody Mary is wearing off. Possibly both." Her gut twisted inside out and Beck groaned.

"Let's get you to the couch." Kris phased away the broken glass and then half lifted, half hobbled with her to the floral print sofa. The trip across the room was all it had taken to get Beck in a full-out sweat.

"I'd better call Achilles."

Beck grabbed her arm. "No. Don't. Let him do whatever big important vampire thing he's doing. I don't like him being around when I'm sick."

"Honey, nobody does," she said as she grabbed the mauve chenille throw from the arm of the couch and tucked it around Beck. "But right now there's only one person you need to get you through this, and it's your mentor."

Kris closed her eyes, her chest expanding with a deep inhale. The air in the room seemed to vibrate slightly in a way that prickled the hairs along Beck's skin.

In the space of two heartbeats, a cloud of dark smoke appeared out of nowhere, swirling and knitting into a human shape. Before those familiar green eyes and killer smile appeared, Beck knew it was Achilles, just by the sheer size of him, that and the big bad black Doc Martens on his feet.

"Is it feeding time?" His lips tipped up at the edges in a concerned smile and despite the increasing pain that rumbled and pulled inside her, Beck's heart flipped.

"Just a touch of tummy trouble." His quirked eyebrow told her more clearly than words that he knew she was telling a whopper. She put some backbone in her voice. "I'll be fine. Really."

He lifted his brow higher. "Am I really that bad of a mentor, fledgling? I thought I'd already covered the basics. Blood equals survival. No blood. No survival. Time to eat."

Beck groaned, not from pain alone. "Please, not another cocktail. I barely gagged down that Bloody Mary you made me."

Kris patted Beck on the shoulder. "Listen to your mentor and it'll go much easier." She turned her gaze to Achilles as she got up from the couch. "I'm going to leave you to care for your fledgling. Let me know how she does." With that Kris vaporized into nothingness on the spot.

Beck stood up, the blanket falling to her feet. For a second she stopped breathing, then it came back in sawing, painful breaths, as if she'd been sprinting. "How'd she do that?"

"Transporting. We'll cover it later. Right now, first things first." His mouth settled into a serious line. "First blood will bring out your fangs, but your body still hasn't fully transitioned." He cocked his head to the side as if listening intently. The dark centers of his eyes grew larger. "You still have a heartbeat. Whatever was in that vaccine was enough to start the process but not enough to finish it. You're stuck in your transition until you get some additional ichor in your system."

A wave of nausea and pain crested over her, pushing her to her knees as she wrapped an arm around her middle. She rocked back and forth, her skin damp with sweat, heart beating too hard in her chest. "I don't care why it is at this point, what do we have to do to make it stop?"

"You need to feed."

"Yeah, yeah. I got that, professor. Where's the glass?"

"No glass." He gently helped her up from the floor.

"What?"

He grinned, his teeth transitioning from normal to pointed as his fangs descended and elongated with an audible *flick*. "It's time to take your fangs on a test drive."

He ran his fangs along the edge of his thick wrist cutting a line that welled with black ichor.

A terrible pressure built on either side of her mouth, near the top of her gum line and Beck could feel something pushing forward, sliding through the soft gum tissue. The tip of her tongue confirmed her personal set of pointed tips were primed and ready. Beck's stomach bucked and kicked, an animal inside that demanded to be fed.

He held out his wrist to her. "Drink."

Beck reared back. "Eewww. No!" A wave of heat swamped over her, an insistent throbbing built just behind her eyes and her body ached. Since when did being hungry feel like the flu?

"Before you reject it out of hand, perhaps you ought to taste it." He dipped the tip of his finger into the black liquid and offered it to her. It gleamed on his finger. She couldn't drag her gaze from it.

Beck's mind was repulsed but her body had other ideas. The sweet scent of black licorice, filled her nose. While other women might swoon for chocolate, black licorice had always been Beck's downfall.

She closed her eyes and tentatively touched the tip of her tongue against his finger. The initial taste of anise was quickly followed by the sensation of liquid heat that shimmered over her tongue, leaving it tingling.

She flicked her eyes open and looked up at the golden good looks of her personal mentor. "Not as bad as I thought." Her tongue moved in quick swipe over her upper lip and one fang.

"Will you trust me now?"

She shrugged, her belly giving an especially large growl that echoed in the room. "Do I have a choice?"

"Pay attention, fledgling. To feed, you need to puncture a sizable artery." He reached out and pressed his fingers against her neck. "The best points are here and here." His fingers traveled down her body, then skimmed lightly along her inner thigh making her contract with need. She inhaled deeply to steady her racing pulse and found the air spiked with a heady combination of rosemary and mint and something else definitely male. She couldn't identify it easily, but it pulled at her like a drug.

"That's if you need a hit fast and a good quantity. For average feeding you could also feast from the vein in the wrist." His fingers brushed the sensitized skin of her own wrist. "Or you could pick any of a dozen other pulse points." His gaze dipped down to her breasts and Beck sucked in a breath as the tips hardened in response to his hungry look.

This lesson was a lot harder to concentrate on than she'd anticipated. Her fangs were actually throbbing.

"Perhaps we should start with a wrist. Come closer."

Beck stepped forward, an invisible cord attached in the area of her belly button, inexorably pulling her toward him. He reached forward, wrapping his uncut arm around her shoulder and turned her so that her back snugged up against his massive chest. The solid heat of him seeped through her clothes and the subtle smell of licorice circulating in the air teased her senses.

Achilles held his thick forearm out before her, the

swell of the dark ichor at his wrist glistening in the overhead lights. Beck was shaking, her skin fevered.

"Don't think, just do it." His husky whisper in her ear shot a shiver of desire rocketing down her spine. Beck closed her eyes and leaned forward, letting her tongue reach out blindly toward the source of the delicious licorice scent.

She lapped once, and a glorious liquid heat shimmered down her throat leaving a fiery trail. Had this been a week ago she would have thought someone had given her a sip of fine aged anisette liquor. But now she knew better. Unable to watch, she closed her eyes, slightly embarrassed, she took another swipe with her tongue.

Achilles nearly fell to his knees at the sensation of her warm tongue on his skin. It sure as hell didn't help that the curve of her bottom was pressing back against his groin as she leaned forward to feed.

Focus, soldier. She's your fledgling.

He swallowed hard, fighting back the fierce tide of longing pulling at him.

"Good. Now use your fangs." A warm appreciative sound rumbled in the back of her throat. Aw, hell. It was a good thing she wasn't feeding from a major artery. "Gently, I don't want my arm ripped open."

The subtle scrape of her tips against his flesh made his skin tighten and ache in unison from head to toe. He backed up from her slightly hoping she was too hungry to notice the rock hard ridge pressed up against her backside. The pop of her fangs sinking into his skin made every nerve come alive, a pure current of ecstasy flowing from the point where they connected through his veins straight to his heart.

Achilles pulled away from the jolt. It was too much. This was more than feeding a fledgling. A glowing ephemeral strand had formed between them. No one else would see it, but he could sense it all the same. Her fangs slipped from his skin as he eased his arm away from her.

"Wait. I'm not finished." She turned her head and gazed at him, her eyes fever bright, her skin luminous. Her pink tongue darted out, swirling over the end of a pearly fang.

Oh, gods. No. She was imprinting with him.

"You've had enough."

A hurt look softened her eyes for a moment but was quickly replaced by something he feared more.

Fierce determination radiated from her so that she nearly glowed with it. She began moving toward him with a fluid seductive sway to her hips like a cat stalking prey. "I'm still hungry."

The vampire pheromones drifted off her, strong, seductive and mixed with her unique blend of ginger and citrus that drove him crazy with thoughts of how the dips and hollows of her would taste. Before she'd begun to transform she'd been hard to resist. But with the power of his ichor saturating her system, she was lethal to his common sense.

This was why mentors were to be unyielding, hardened more than any other vampire. To resist the temptation she offered took nerves of titanium.

She lifted her chin, lips lightly parted, her fangs brushing the fullness of her supple bottom lip. "Achilles," she breathed, "come to me."

Chapter 8

Achilles was helpless to resist her.

She slid her small hands up his chest, wrapping her arms around his neck, pressing herself against him from breast to thigh. Her body heat seared everywhere they touched. "Feed me." She might as well have said *take me*. Either way it had the same impact on him. Achilles's legs trembled. His body ached to feel her.

A low determined rumble from her stomach indicated she wasn't just reacting to the imprint forming between them, she was indeed still hungry. Achilles blew out a ragged breath. He didn't need the damn oxygen in his body but maintaining control was essential to his survival and hers.

It was his duty to feed her, to protect her, no matter what it cost him personally.

And that cost was going to be high.

Incredibly high.

Forming a full imprint with her would mean he'd be excommunicated from the clan. It was one thing to exist as a halfling, unable to feel the things others took for granted; it was completely another to be excommunicated from the clan.

Vampires like that had few options and either became solitary or part of a nest of reivers to survive. Life as a solitary vampire was impossible for a halfling. He'd go mad without interacting with others of his kind. And adopting the mores of a nesting vampire went against everything within him.

No. That wasn't an option, either. If it came down to being excommunicated, he'd beg Dmitri to behead him. But at this moment none of that mattered. What mattered was taking care of his fledgling, the cost be damned.

He looked down into her eyes and found himself in the cool tranquility of a shaded wood. "Then eat." The words came out with a slight tremor, because, despite the fear of what might happen, his need was almost as intense as hers.

Her fingers threaded through the hair at his nape, her small palm curving to cup the back of his head. She pressed his head down at the same time she rose up on her toes to bring them face-to-face.

"Kiss me."

Achilles couldn't stifle the primal growl vibrating deep in his chest. He captured her mouth, fangs and all, in a fierce kiss, his hands splaying over the curve of her hips. Her soft wet mouth against him sent sparks shooting through him like an electrical hot wire.

The dewy tongue that had been torturous before now brushed with a tempting silken slide that made him lose all his good intentions. Her scent blended with the nuance of his own ichor, making her taste like a sweet confection impossible to resist.

He crushed her to him, reveling in the feel of her firm, hard-tipped breasts pressed against the wall of his chest. The soft sound she made deep in her throat torqued his lust yet another notch. And he knew, he feared, that every second, every sensation, bound them more tightly together, creating a stronger, unbreakable imprint.

Mind-blowing as kissing Rebecca was, Achilles tried to pull back. The warning bells in his brain were pealing loud and clear. He knew, as she couldn't, the ramifications of taking this to the next level. Deep in the recesses of his mind he was conscious of what was really happening between them and his duty to stop it.

Her strength had increased and Achilles found himself locked in her arms. She moved swiftly. Her fangs scraped along the tender inside of his lip as she suckled it, releasing a flood of ichor into his mouth. She kissed, still sucking at his lip, her tongue touching and twirling with his.

You have to stop. You must stop. Kill the imprint. Kill it now, his rational mind screamed. But gods, how could he release her when she felt so damn perfect in his arms? When for the first time in centuries had he felt awake, alive? All he could think was how good it would be to bond with this woman.

But she doesn't want to be a vampire. That thought stopped him in his tracks. He pulled back, swiping roughly at the remaining ichor seeping from the cuts already healing in his lip.

"That's enough, fledgling. No more."

Rebecca tipped up her chin, licking her bee-stung lips, dark from their kiss, with relish. "It's no big deal." Hazel eyes gleamed with excitement. "A kiss, that's all."

If she only knew. He could already feel the throbbing of the imprint in the air between them. Perhaps she didn't know what that sensation was, but he damn well knew. And he knew better than to allow this to continue.

He pulled away, shoving down the sleeve of his sweater over his forearm. "You should have plenty of ichor to see you through a full transition."

"Meaning what?" Beck touched her fingers to her sensitive lips.

He crossed the room and sprawled out on her girly couch. Wasn't easy trying to maintain a light casual air between them as if what had transpired had really meant nothing at all. Just dinner—vampire-style. "You won't need to feed from me again."

"Ever?"

He shook his head, grateful for the moment that there was some space between them. "Regular blood should do the trick from here on out. I'll teach you how to glamour and feed properly from a donor." Beck pressed her two fingers to the spot between her eyes then spread them upward along the ridge so they spread out in a V just over her brows.

Unable to take his gaze from her face, Achilles sat up his eyes narrowed. "How long have you done that?"

"What?"

"That. With your fingers."

Beck stared at him. "I still don't get what you're asking."

He mimicked her movement showing her precisely what he'd seen. "That."

She shrugged. "I don't know. Always."

Gods above and below. For an instant she had reminded him so clearly of Ione.

In all his years as a mentor, only Ione had been able to break his concentration, his focus, with a sensual pull so deep it couldn't be denied.

But imprints were eternal, lasting beyond the boundaries of time or space, life, death and undeath. How could he possibly be open to forming an imprint with Rebecca when he'd clearly formed one with Ione thousands of years before? His bond with Ione had lasted centuries and had nearly been the death of him.

But his attraction to Rebecca was no less real, no less addictive. If he were honest with himself and her as well, he hadn't merely marked her as his own when they'd kissed while she had dreamed. The imprint had begun to form the moment they'd physically touched and she'd wrapped her arms around his neck. It had only strengthened when she'd fed from him.

He'd done his best to deny it. But an imprint was

something beyond the powers of an individual vampire. It was the combined powers, passions and pain of two vampires forever linked.

The realization hit with the force of a category five hurricane, leaving him shaken and in a cold sweat.

No. *Impossible…*

And yet—

Could it be that the reason he couldn't resist Rebecca was because she was Ione reborn?

As a warrior he should have seen the signs. But the knowledge was both bitter and sweet. Ione may have been reborn as vampires with unfinished business sometimes were, but in this lifetime as Rebecca she had no intention of remaining a vampire. Worse yet, in this century she had the technology to make it so.

As painful as severing the newly reformed imprint would be, allowing it to strengthen would only cause them both more pain when she returned to her mortal form. Half of him, and of her, would die. He'd been there, lived that and wouldn't put his worst enemy through it, let alone Rebecca.

He raised a hand to touch her, but let it drop useless by his side. Beck turned away, her shoulders tipped inward. She believed he'd rejected her. *It's for the best,* he told himself resolutely. *Do your job, let her go. Let the imprint die. Maybe in another time and another place, she'll come back again and want to be a vampire.*

"My head just hurts," she muttered.

"Is your vision shifting?"

Rebecca's eyes narrowed, then blinked rapidly as

if dust had been blown into them making them water. "What's happening to me?" An intensity sparkled in her voice. She plunked down on the couch, holding her hand out in front of her and twisted it first one way then the other, testing her vision.

"It's all part of the final stages of your transition."

He grabbed the remote and flipped on the television to reinforce the casual image he was going for. In reality his sudden realization about Ione being reborn as Rebecca had him feeling more skittish than a yearling colt brought out into the ring for its first war horse training. Ione had been the mentor, he the fledgling. Now with the roles reversed he was bound and determined not to repeat their earlier mistake. He would protect them both against the unendurable pain—even if it meant hiding the truth about the imprint from Rebecca. Even if that meant rejecting her advances.

He didn't know what was on the television, hadn't even glanced at it. He was just staring in the general direction of the screen so he wouldn't have to make eye contact with her. His ears strained and heard the ebbing pace of her heart, the beats coming slower and slower. Did she even realize that she was losing her last grasp on her mortality? What surprised him more was that she hadn't seemed to need to sleep in the earth to complete her transition the way most vampires did. The mutated virus in her system was odd, indeed.

"Stop spoon-feeding me, Achilles. Isn't it your job to explain things to me and help me with this transition? Tell me how to stop whatever's happening!"

"You can't stop it. Your senses are becoming amplified. Sight, smell, hearing, taste—all amplified a thousandfold."

She shifted, leaning forward. "What about touch?"

Unable to stop it, his gaze flicked to hers and held. "Yeah. That, too." She stretched, hands high over her head, causing her neck to arch and her breasts to thrust proudly forward. Gods, she was gorgeous. Gorgeous, dangerous and totally, completely off-limits.

Beck relaxed out of her stretch more energized that she had been in years. Whatever was in that ichor was amazing stuff. A bit freaky at first, but amazing. After she completed the vaccine, she fully intended to explore the medicinal properties of ichor. She did a slow mental check of all her systems, filing away what she noted so she could share it with Margo when they spoke again.

Her breath caught. "Wait. I don't have a pulse!" She patted herself down as if it were somehow misplaced in one pocket or another.

Achilles sat casually in the recliner, phased a beer in hand and raised it in salute to her. He gave a dry chuckle completely unimpressed by the gravity of the situation. "Congratulations, you've joined the ranks of the undead." He turned back to the television and took a sip.

Her fangs throbbed again, but this time was different. The gnawing hunger had abated. But she was pissed, her breath came fast and heavy, the air smelling oddly of pepper. She hadn't asked to be a vampire, had never wanted to be undead. Being congratulated and reminded only stung more. She needed to stop being such a sissy and get back to work on the vaccine. She needed to find a way to get a hold of ichor from Evaline St. Croix.

"You can stop huffing and puffing like you're a fire-breathing dragon, as well." The deep masculine tone of his voice was laced with annoyed amusement. "You won't need to breathe unless it makes you feel more comfortable around mortals."

"I'll keep breathing if I feel like it."

He shrugged. "Your choice. I was just letting you know it was unnecessary."

How's the fledgling holding up? The voice came out of nowhere, echoing in her head just like Achilles had when he'd been talking to her vampire to vampire. Only this wasn't Achilles's voice. It sounded like Dmitri.

Then she heard Achilles respond. *Good. She's finally transitioned.*

Congratulations. You got her through it.

Beck swung her gaze across the room focusing on Achilles. With a start she realized she was hearing the private mental exchange between him and Dmitri. Even with the suddenly guilty dip in her stomach at the thought that she was eavesdropping, this was too important. She screwed her eyes shut and tried to tune in, or mind meld, or whatever it was vampires did.

Don't congratulate me just yet. I think we might have a worse problem to deal with, and it may be something I need your help to resolve.

Exactly how did she get through her transition? I thought it had stalled.

She needed ichor.

Saints. Brother—tell me you didn't feed her.

What else was I suppose to do, let her die?

Dmitri let out an irritated sigh that echoed in her head. *You know I have to ask you this, have you imprinted with her?*

The long pause made her stomach squeeze and turn uncomfortably. What was an imprint and how dangerous was it? The way Dmitri sounded, it seemed like a very big no-no, which meant it couldn't be good.

Yes.

Hell. You'd better bring her to my office at headquarters. I've got news regarding the lead on Rebecca's maker.

Beck's eyes popped open, but she didn't dare look in Achilles's direction for fear of revealing that she'd been listening in. Dear God. What did it all mean?

Suddenly he was no longer on the couch. Instead he was right beside her, his words close enough to send a shiver of longing down her spine. "We're leaving. Get your jacket."

Beck crossed her arms and turned to face him. "It's almost dawn. I don't think that's such a good idea. Vampires and sunlight don't exactly mix, do they?"

"You're right. Grab your sunglasses, too."

"I fail to see how that'd help me from burning to a crisp."

He heaved a sigh and materialized her sunglasses into his hand. "You won't fry, just possibly get a nasty sunburn. But from the looks of your skin, it wouldn't be anything you haven't risked before." He unfolded the glasses and gently slid them on her face. "The sunglasses will delay getting a migraine from the intensity of the light."

"But how—"

He pressed a cool broad finger to her lips, making them tingle. "You can ask questions later. Right now we have an appointment to keep. I'll drive."

He phased a fitted black leather jacket and a pair of ultra black wraparound sunglasses for himself and her wool peacoat. He walked her to the door and opened it. "After you."

She looked at the open door. "Why are we going in the car when you could just zap us there?"

"It's called transporting, and we're going in the car because I *like* driving the car."

"What was Dmitri talking about?"

He stared at her long and hard, a glint of wariness in his eyes. "Well, well. Eavesdropping at such a tender age for a vampire. That's a new one."

She cocked her hip to the side and crossed her arms. "What is an imprint?"

She couldn't see his eyes behind his dark sunglasses that all but screamed *screw you*. "Imprint?"

"Yes."

"Something you don't need to worry about because you're planning to go back to being mortal. Right?"

"Damn right." Beck twisted her tongue in her mouth gnawing on the edge of it. Against her better judgment she grasped his arm. "Perhaps I want to know for scientific reasons."

"Perhaps you want to know because you're nosy." Beneath her fingers his arm flexed. God his muscles were huge.

"Look, I think I have the right if there's something growing, forming, building, whatever between us."

He pulled his sunglasses down and his intense gaze hit her dead center in the chest. "Right now the only thing between us is a relationship as mentor and fledgling. Once you go back to being mortal, even that will cease to exist, and I'll just be a figment of your imagination."

More like her sexual fantasies. She glanced down at her hand on his arm and realized he hadn't removed it. His jaw was working hard, and she could hear his teeth grinding as if he held an awful lot back. The hot blatantly sexual energy coming off him hit her. She looked up through her lashes at him. "So do you feed all your fledglings like that?"

"No."

Beck quirked a brow, her lips bending into a small warm smile. "Then I'm special."

"Yes."

His voice sounded thick. Her fangs throbbed just behind her gums at his response. Clearly he didn't ever intend to tell her this, but she still wanted something from him. She wanted him to explain the imprint to her rather than just brush off her questions as if she were stupid.

"You want something, Achilles. I can see it in your

eyes and feel it through our touch. What do you want from me?"

He gently, but firmly pulled her hand from his arm, leaving her feeling the loss as if she'd suddenly snapped her mooring and was now adrift in an unfamiliar ocean.

"Nothing. Not a damn thing." With that he turned on his heel and strode out into the dawn, leaving her to follow.

Chapter 9

They headed downtown, winding through early morning rush-hour traffic. The streetlights were still lit as they drove, and they cast the edges of his face in hard planes of light and shadow. The dark sunglasses only added to his Terminatorlike appearance. Achilles's hot and cold response left her confused and the inside of the Veyron sparked with tension.

Beck knew she hadn't merely imagined the sexual chemistry between them. It was there. It was palpable, and it was eating her alive.

"Where are we going?" She said it more to break the tension than because she had the need to know.

"The entrance to the Cascade Clan headquarters is through the Seattle Underground."

"You mean that cheesy underground tour in Pioneer Square?"

Even with the sunglasses in place, she could feel the burning point of his stare as he shifted his head to gaze in her direction. "Not everything is what it looks like on the surface."

"Since when did you get to be so profound, professor?"

He turned back to face the road. "Since I got landed with you, Doc."

He made her sound like an unwanted burden. A small uncomfortable bubble welled up in the pit of her stomach. He swung the car into a parking structure and headed for the lower levels.

"We'll park here and walk the rest of the way in."

Beck pulled off her sunglasses and looked around. The rest of the way turned out to be a service entrance to the side of the elevators. The bland gray metal door blended in so well, it was nearly indistinguishable from the concrete around it.

"So this is the front door?"

He stared at her, his glasses masking his eyes as he reached for the doorknob and shoved a key in the lock. "You were expecting doormen?"

Beck shrugged. "Is Evaline St. Croix here?"

His hand stopped midtwist. "Why do you want to know?"

"Professional curiosity. I want to meet the person who's the genetic antiviral."

He opened the door and held it for her. "Do you ever take a vacation?"

Beck stepped past him and into what she recognized as an elevator. "Not if I can help it." He shut the outer door and the elevator door closed with a metallic shush.

Achilles pulled a key card from his pocket and slid it through the reader slot by the button panel. "You need to learn to relax, Doc."

Beck snorted and crossed her arms. "You're one to lecture. When was the last time you took a vacation?"

He poked the button leading to the bottom level and then slipped off his sunglasses. "Soldiers don't take holidays."

"Neither do scientists," she shot back.

The doors opened and they stepped out into a modern atrium of sorts created from white walls and chrome fixtures with a high lighted ceiling of translucent glass. Lots of green plants clustered around empty sitting areas of comfortable white couches and chairs. Across the room a delicate waterfall bubbled down a wall of gray stones, the whispering sound of it amplified in the wide-open area. Off to the left was a receptionist's desk with a woman dressed in white scrubs, her brown hair in a twist. Near the desk stood a security officer suited out in black. He was nearly as big as Achilles, but one look at him said he had far less humor.

The scent of clean cotton, green plants and some kind of artificially floral air freshener tickled Beck's nose. In any other setting it might have seemed serene. To Beck it seemed surreal. They were underground, beneath the waking city of Seattle and nobody, except the vampires, knew it even existed. "Nice place."

Achilles jerked his head to the side. "That desk is the reception and security point to our medical facility and laboratories. Once we've met with Dmitri, perhaps he can arrange for you to have a tour and get answers to some of your questions. Right now, we're going directly to Dmitri's offices. Follow me."

He turned down a hall papered in a sage green leaf pattern punctuated by beautiful paintings and artistic color photographs. It looked just like any other hall in a high-end set of office high-rises in downtown Seattle. The hall ended at a set of frosted double glass doors. Achilles pushed open the door, waiting for her to cross into a reception area with tasteful teak furniture. Behind the reception desk, a woman with shoulder-length black hair wearing a red business suit lifted her head and offered them a bland smile.

"Morning, Ciara." Her smile broadened when she saw that the visitor was Achilles. She winked, before looking over Beck. She sniffed lightly, a slightly confused look flitting across her features before they smoothed back into flawless perfection once more as she turned back to Achilles.

"And this is?"

"Dr. Rebecca Chamberlin."

The receptionist nodded. "Go right in, he's waiting for you both."

Achilles gave her a curt nod and grasped Beck's hand, pulling her with him toward the dark office door before them. His touch was warm, dry and smooth, but still sent a zap of high-octane sexual energy shimmering up her arm. Totally the wrong time and definitely the wrong place. But in all her life, Beck had never felt this close, this fast, to someone. It was as if he knew her, as if he was the secret missing ingredient in a chemical formula that made up relationships she'd never been able to figure out.

Dmitri, dark and brooding behind his massive burl desk, didn't look nearly as casual as Beck remembered him. He was in a power suit that snugged along his broad shoulders topped off with a crisp black shirt and a red tie. He glanced up when they entered.

"You took long enough, brother." His words weren't loaded with malice, but were edgy just the same.

Achilles braced his feet apart and faced Dmitri head-on. "You said you had news."

Dmitri glanced at Beck, and she felt cold sluice over her head, down her back and shoulders as if someone had dumped a bucket of frigid water over her. "We know who Rebecca's maker is."

"And?"

The brown of his eyes darkened to nearly black, as he turned his gaze back to Achilles. "It's what we feared."

"Vane."

Dmitri nodded, leaning forward and planting his fists down on the top of his desk. "The council has convened a meeting. They want us there in two hours."

She didn't know who or what the council was, but

she knew Vane meant trouble. The situation and the tension ebbing and flowing around the two mountain-sized men in her presence were enough to make her feel light-headed and off balance. "What are we going to do until then?"

Achilles slid his gaze to hers. "We wait here."

"If we're just waiting, do you think I could meet Evaline St. Croix?"

Dmitri's gaze flicked to Achilles, his brow raising.

What does she want with Eva? Beck heard Dmitri's voice loud and clear as though he spoke to her, but knew she was once again listening in to his mental communication with Achilles since his dark eyes weren't even looking at her.

Something about researching a natural antivirus.

Dmitri sighed. *Yeah, Kris gave me a difficult time about our intentions to wipe out the vaccine project completely. Something about people having a choice.*

Beck couldn't stop herself. "They should have a choice," she said defiantly. "I would've liked a choice. And there is no reason why vampires and humans can't live peaceably just because there is an option for those who need it."

Both vampires stared at her, Dmitri's eyes slightly wider. "She's already reading others?"

Achilles nodded. "Would have told you, but only just found out myself."

Dmitri pinned her with the hard unyielding gaze of a man used to the responsibility and right of power. "The vaccine poses a risk to our kind."

But Beck had been challenged by far bigger blowhards her whole life. "All science is a calculated risk. Just because something is risky doesn't mean you give up on it."

Dmitri glanced at Achilles. "She's got a good head on her shoulders."

Achilles grinned. "I'd like to take the credit for that as her mentor, but she came with that before I got to her."

Dmitri nodded. "I'll see what I can do to get a hold of Eva."

He sat down behind his desk, a silent gesture of dismissal, and Achilles grasped her arm steering her out of the office. "Time to go, Doc."

He walked with her out of the offices and back down the hall toward the atrium. "What does it mean that Vane is my maker?"

Achilles's steps faltered. "He's not your maker in the traditional sense. He didn't feed you himself."

"Like you did."

Achilles's jaw flexed. "Yes. Like I did. But he is the one whose ichor you used in your vaccine. There is a connection there which Dmitri believes set him off to track you at the club."

"So we're related?" Her stomach kind of bucked at that one. What if he was also the vampire masquerading around as Victor who had turned her mother?

"In a manner of speaking. Which makes you kin to Dmitri, since he's Vane's blood brother."

"Back up. They're related? He acts like he hates Vane."

"He does. They share the same maker, Larissa, but like you, Dmitri never intended to be a vampire. He actually used to hunt them in the Middle Ages. Now he's our *Trejan,* our Vice President of sorts, second in command of the entire clan."

Beck shook her head. "That's certainly a switch."

Achilles's shoulders stiffened. "We may not all decide to come to this existence in the same way, but it's what you do with what you've been given, not how you were given it, that defines you."

"Thanks, professor, I'll remember that," she quipped. "Are you sure you weren't a Greek philosopher rather than a solider?"

He raised an eyebrow looking as though she'd insulted him.

Beck got the sense that she had drifted into dangerous territory digging up his past and quickly started walking toward the atrium. "What about caffeine? Do vampires drink coffee, tea, diet soda? Right now I'm feeling severely caffeine deprived. Do you have a vending machine around here somewhere?"

Achilles caught up with her in three quick strides, his legs far longer than her own. "You're not hungry are you?"

She slid a cautious glance sideways at him. "I just need caffeine."

They found a quiet table and he phased a cup of steaming coffee for each of them. "You like cream or sugar?"

"Both."

The contents of her cup swirled, turning paler. She hadn't managed to materialize anything the time or two she'd tried, but perhaps she wasn't doing it right. As cool a skill as it was, she wanted to be successful at it once, before she went back to being human, just to see how it felt to create something from nothing.

A curl of smokelike air in one of the two empty chairs at their table quickly knitted together into the form of a woman with long wavy chestnut hair close to Beck's own color, but with far fewer red highlights, and big pale blue eyes. A softly knit purple wrap hung loosely over her slender shoulders.

"Could you get me some, too? Black with sugar?" she asked, her wide mouth forming into a generous smile as she held a hand out to Beck in greeting. "Sorry to pop in like this, but Dmitri said you wanted to see me as soon as possible. I'm Eva."

Beck shook her hand. A third cup appeared on the table along with a plate of crisp beignets coated with a dusting of powdered sugar. Eva's grin grew wider. "You remembered! Thank you, Achilles." The yeasty scent of the freshly fried pastries caused Beck's mouth to water.

"Fresh from Café du Monde." Achilles took a sip of his coffee.

Eva picked one up and took a bite, closing her eyes and licking the powdered sugar from her lips.

Beck snatched up a beignet and took a bite, as well. Damn, they were good.

"So you're curious about me." Eva's words stopped

Beck midway through her bite. She need a second to think how to handle her request for some of Eva's ichor so she just stuffed the entire thing in her mouth and nodded as she chewed.

Achilles spoke first. "Rebecca is a scientist. She thinks you may be the key to something very important she's working on."

Eva glanced at him. "This is because of the whole salvation thing, isn't it?"

He nodded.

"Did you have a maker?" Beck asked quickly.

Eva turned her gaze to Beck. "No. I didn't. I became a vampire by a rather unconventional means. I wasn't expected to survive, and yet somehow I did."

"That's why I think hidden in your ichor may be the genetic key I've been searching for."

"For what?"

Beck threw a cautious glance at Achilles. *Should I tell Eva about the vaccine?*

Achilles nodded once in the affirmative.

She leveled her gaze at Eva. "I was turned into a vampire by some unconventional means myself. A vaccine that I was developing to help protect humans from accidentally becoming vampires wasn't as viable as we'd hoped. I believe it's because we're missing whatever the something is that you possess. The key that will give both vampires and humans options to choose how they want to live their lives."

Eva leaned in closer. "What can I do to help you?"

"I'd like a sample of your ichor for testing, to see

what genetic markers may differ from the DNA in our original ichor base."

Eva stared at Beck, her blue eyes intense. "When I was twenty-one, a palm reader told me my fate was to change the world. I thought that had already happened when I saved the vampire race from extinction. Looks like I wasn't quite finished yet. I'll do it. I'll have a sample waiting for you by this evening at the medical center here in the clan complex."

Beck grabbed Eva's hand, it was smooth and warm. "Thank you, Eva. I can't tell you how valuable this could be to our research. I appreciate it."

Eva nodded. "We all have a role to play in this world." She gave a slight shrug. "I guess mine is to help save others."

Across the table from the women, Achilles stiffened. His sudden shift in manner immediately drew Beck's attention.

"What's wrong?"

"It's time to go before the council."

Beck's stomach dropped down to the vicinity of her shoes. Eva's other hand covered Beck's and she gave a slight squeeze of reassurance. "They aren't as scary as they seem. You're with Achilles. I'm sure everything will work out for the best."

And as quickly as Eva had appeared, she vanished, as did her coffee and the rest of the beignets.

"Just keep quiet and let me do the talking," Achilles instructed as they made their way toward the council chamber deep in the heart of the clan complex.

His words set her off in all the wrong ways, but deep down Beck knew it was sound advice. Never having met a vampire council she didn't exactly understand how it all fit together with his world, now her world for the moment.

"Are they like the Supreme Court or something?"

"Similar. They guide all the laws of the council and share responsibility for administering those laws along with the laird of our clan, Roman Petrov."

"So this isn't something minor."

"Hardly. The council only gathers to determine serious matters. Roman will be seated in the center with the other eight council members gathered around him."

Beck swallowed. In school she'd been the quiet studious one, and had never been called to the principal's office. Somehow just the sensation of being the root of serious trouble made her nauseous.

She got up and followed Achilles to the council chambers. At the entrance enormous, intricately carved black doors sported three red interlocked circles and were centered in a wall of chiseled black rock. The only light came from above, casting the faces of the massive guards dressed in black uniforms on either side in dark shadows.

Beck noticed each of the guards glance at Achilles and give him a barely perceptible nod of deference. He had said he was captain of security for the clan. Perhaps these men were under his command. If so, the fact that they respected him, despite his being called before a council for some supposed major infraction, spoke highly of him.

Achilles inhaled, his chest expanding, his shoulders pulled down and back, making him look even more imposing. He glanced down at her beside him. "Ready, Doc?"

Hell, no. But what choice did she have? The only reassurance she had was that he was right beside her, imposing, strong and definitely on her side. Beck nodded, her throat too thick to speak. She resisted the sudden urge to reach out and put her hand in his much larger one.

The guards pushed back the daunting doors and she walked in a step behind Achilles. High on the walls candles flickered in the ornately scrolled wrought iron candelabras, casting shadows on the crimson velvet that curtained large portions of the dark rock walls.

Nine carved cherry-wood chairs sat in a semicircle around a raised, black-tiled dais with an odd interlinked three-circle mark. The design's red rock contrasted with the surrounding black stone. Beck looked deeply into the eyes of the vampires seated in each of nine chairs.

Several looked positively ancient with long white hair, thin and fine as candy floss, and deeply hooded red eyes hidden in folds of paper-thin skin. Others had pale eyes, that same shade of gray that had flashed in Achilles's eyes. The effect was startling and more than intimidating. The air crackled with power.

At the center sat one of the three vampires who didn't have odd colored eyes. Instead his eyes were so dark they were nearly all pupil, and seemed soulless to Beck. Maybe it's because they all are soulless and undead, she thought. She choked a little, unable to stifle a cough that tickled at the back of throat.

Since he was in the middle, Beck guessed that the vampire with the intense dark eyes was Roman, Laird of the Cascade Clan. He sat at the center in a slightly larger chair, four council members in smaller matching chairs on either side of him. With a gliding motion of his hand, Roman indicated she and Achilles should step up onto the dais.

"We have heard evidence that your fledgling was made by the reiver known as Vane. She's also been implicated in the development of a product intended to disrupt the creation of new vampires. With such affiliations, she's a danger to our clan. She can't be trusted." His voice echoed in the chamber, reverberating in Beck's chest and making her feel even more hollow inside. She was suddenly incredibly grateful that Achilles was standing there beside her. A golden knight amid a very dark assembly.

"With respect, my Laird, bloodline alone is not enough to condemn a vampire," Achilles responded his tone firm but even. "She'd never even met Vane prior to the start of her transition. The ichor came to her through an anonymous third person and was only administered accidentally to her without her consent."

"How do you know you can trust her?" One of the vampires with long white hair asked. He had gray eyes so pale they seemed nearly white.

Achilles shifted his stance, stepping slightly closer to her and turned to the older council member. "She's mine."

"That's a bold statement coming from a mentor," one of the red-eyed vampires said, his short dark hair making his skin seem all the paler.

"She's mine *to protect*," he amended, suddenly very aware of the eyes of the council boring into him as he stood in front of Rebecca. "Vane has no claim to her as a maker. He doesn't even realize that his ichor is the one that was used in the original vaccine, let alone that it unintentionally caused Dr. Chamberlin to partially transition."

"Partially?"

"My lords of the council, the transition wasn't complete. The genetic manipulation of the ichor in Dr. Chamberlin's experiments caused the beginning of a transition, but wasn't complete enough for her to finish it. She required additional ichor."

"And who donated this ichor to her?" Fury underscored Roman's tone.

His gut curled in upon itself. Achilles knew his next words were as close to a confession of an imprint as he could come without spitting out the word. No matter how noble his intentions, if they wanted to excommunicate him from the clan, it would be fully within their rights.

"I did, my lords. It was that, or as a mentor watch my fledgling die."

The council members bent their heads together deep in discussion, blocking their thoughts from him. Roman glanced at them all, waiting until their attention was once again fixed on the two standing on the dais. "As a mentor you are charged with doing all you can to protect and guide your fledgling in their transition and training. For this we approve the decision you made to give ichor to your fledgling. However, be aware that should an imprint form between the two of you, there will be a full council convened to discuss your excommunication from this clan."

Achilles resisted the overwhelming urge to glance in Rebecca's direction. "I am aware of that risk, my lords, and the consequences should I fail."

Roman stood, the weight of his words spearing straight through Achilles to his most vulnerable part. "You may continue to train your fledgling, but be aware Vane will not rest until he has claimed her."

The thought of Vane even glancing in Rebecca's direction caused anger, hot and acidic, to well up within him. He closed his eyes for an instant. Despite Vane, he knew who the bigger threat was to his fledgling. Himself. At that moment he hated himself for his own weakness. Spartans did away with the weak.

If he allowed the imprint to fully form and she transitioned back into a mortal form, he'd never get her back again. He'd forever be a halfling. He'd be excommunicated. It made death look damn inviting.

"My lords, you know I have suffered for my past choices." Two of the vampires with long white hair nodded knowingly. "I respectfully request that should it ever come to a point where you would decide to excommunicate me, that you would behead me instead."

"No!" Rebecca shouted. It echoed in the great cavern of the council chamber.

He glanced at her only briefly. She had no idea what it meant to suffer as he had. She couldn't possibly understand that beheading would be far kinder than slowly going insane with no hope, no love and no release of death to greet you.

Roman ignored Rebecca's outburst. He stood, placing his palms together. "I shall grant your request, Captain. But you realize that if you should fail, the price shall be your head."

Achilles nodded, placing his forearm, fisted close over his chest in a kind of salute. "Thank you for your kindness, my Laird."

He pulled a sputtering Rebecca with him as he stepped down from the dais and exited the chambers. "Kindness? Kindness! He's going to kill you if you screw up!"

He came to a dead stop and looked at her. "Then I'd better not screw up." But a line across his throat burned even as he said the words, because he knew the imprint had already begun. Their only hope was that the good doctor would find a way to become mortal again.

Chapter 10

Later that afternoon they met in a large well-lit gym with old-fashioned wooden bleachers stacked high against one wall and a matted workout area spread over the highly polished wood floor. The only good thing was that unlike the high school gym of her memories, this one smelled of lemon wood polish rather than stinky socks and stale sweat.

For a moment Beck had a high school flashback, only back then there was no way she would have been alone with a guy this hot in the school gym—or anywhere else for that matter. She'd been the science geek. Unfortunately, this hot guy's sole purpose was to make her hot and sweaty in a totally unromantic way.

"Now that you've transitioned and your powers have emerged, it's time for me to train you," Achilles said.

"Just a heads up, Achilles. I was lousy at sports, P.E. and everything else athletic. I don't think I'm going to do any better at vampire boot camp."

Achilles grinned as he pulled at the hem of his black T-shirt, yanking it off over his head in one fluid movement. Beck had only imagined what he'd looked like when she'd felt the rock hard strength beneath his clothes. But clearly her imagination wasn't all that good. He looked even better. She sucked in a startled breath. God, he was sexy as hell.

"I don't have to take off my shirt, too, do I?" she asked, her voice nearly squeaking, her mouth dry as cotton.

His eyes glittered in a way that spoke of pure male interest. "It would be better if you didn't. We have lessons to focus on."

Beck hopped from foot to foot in a slow jog, shaking out her arms. "What's up first, professor?"

He glanced at her feet and she slowed to a stop. "As a vampire you move faster than any mortal."

"Do we have to keep saying mortal? Why can't we call people human?"

"Because technically vampires are human, too. The only difference is the genetic twist that makes us immortal."

Beck nodded but she wasn't paying all that much attention. She'd always been a sucker for a great set of shoulders and muscular arms. Achilles had both in ample amounts. "Fine. You were saying something about moving faster?"

* * *

Achilles rolled his shoulders to take the edge off. It did no good. Being in the training gym with her was a heady experience. Her hair was pulled back in a ponytail, exposing the elegant length of her neck and enticing curve where it smoothed into collarbone. The T-shirt she'd borrowed from Kristin outlined her breasts, dainty waist and the womanly flare of her hips, while the shorts gave him far too good a view of her long silky legs. Gods, she'd make a glorious vampiress.

His ichor moved in a quick rhythm through her veins. Her eyes dilated as her glance bounced from his torso to his eyes. The scent of her vampire pheromones shifted, the deeper jasmine scent becoming more pronounced. Looking at him half-clothed turned her on. Another measure of his reserve crumbled. *Focus, soldier. It doesn't matter if she likes what she sees, get back to the lesson. She is still a threat to you.* He swiped his tongue hard across his upper gum line to soothe the ache of pressing fangs.

"To move faster, push yourself into the movement with focus."

"Kind of like materializing objects?" She nibbled at the side of her bottom lip.

An image of kissing her rose crystal clear in his mind. He squeezed his hand into a fist banishing the image and tried to focus on her training.

"Correct with the same focus."

"So then are you technically materializing yourself to a different place?"

"Must you analyze everything, woman? Can't you just try it?"

"Yes, I must, and no, I need to understand it to do it."

He leaned his head back and stared at the ceiling. Patience. He needed patience and perhaps an entire tub of ice cold water. "The mechanics are basically the same. You're phasing, but it's not the same as transporting."

"Why?"

"Gods!" In a blink he was right up against her. "Perhaps we ought to try it another time. Clearly you aren't ready." The truth was he wasn't prepared for the assault her very presence waged on his senses.

She gave him a wicked smile. "Really?" In a blink she was standing on the top of the empty bleachers. Her grin was wide, and her eyes bright as she punched the air in triumph with both fists, then shook her butt in a mini touchdown dance of her own. "That was a rush."

He nodded in approval. "Sometimes there is no time to think, only time to act."

He watched her move toward him, but it was only because he was a vampire that he glimpsed her quick actions at all. She stood before him now, her full lips bent into a small teasing smile that made him hard. Gods, preventing an imprint with her would be as easy as asking him never to drink blood again. In other words, totally impossible.

"Hey, I'm not even breathing hard."

He brushed back a stray piece of hair that escaped from her messy ponytail and curled down the side of her face. "That's because you aren't breathing," he said drily, releasing her hair.

"What else?"

He wanted to tell her that she was filling the air with vampire pheromones that were knocking him senseless. To tell her that all he could think of was hitting the showers with her in tow and rubbing her down with soap so he could feel the silky slide of it against her bare wet skin. But he didn't dare. Control. Absolute control. Spartan control.

"You also aren't aging."

She slapped at his shoulder. "That's not what I meant. I want to know what else I can do."

"See the top of the bleachers?"

"Yes. I was just there." She grinned with satisfaction and a bit of smugness.

"Let's take a jumping lesson."

He grabbed her hand in his. An electric arc sparked between them. Achilles tried to ignore it, but it was getting harder and harder. "Same focus, only this time picture your destination and think up."

He crouched, the muscles in his legs coiling. She glanced at him and followed his example. "Ready?"

She nodded locking her gaze on his, the hazel a kaleidoscope of changing greens and browns bright with excitement. "On three. One. Two. Three." He launched upward, and she easily followed. They landed together with a solid thud.

They straightened up and Beck let out a burst of excited laughter. "Okay, now, that, *that* was cool."

"See? I told you being a vampire has its perks."

She bounced up on the balls of her feet, enthusiasm vibrating in the air around her. "Can you imagine the implications of what this could do for people if you just knew what genomes were responsible? This could revolutionize medicine."

Rebecca's mind was as alluring as the rest of her. Her intelligence, her desire to know all the answers—no matter what the subject—fascinated Achilles. She was forever thinking, analyzing, prodding and probing. He'd only known one other woman this analytical, this focused. Rebecca was just like Ione in that way.

He shoved the insane comparison away. "Now let's work on your hand-to-hand combat skills." Gods. He was going to have to *touch* her for this. Touch her silky skin, brush against her soft breasts, position her sleek body...

Rebecca heaved a great sigh. "Seriously? When am I ever going to need to fight in hand-to-hand combat?"

He jumped down to the floor mats and she followed, but before she could straighten up from her crouch, he'd rolled her and pinned her to the smooth cold mats. Her hands were locked above her head and her hips were tucked beneath his thighs.

"You think another vampire isn't going to fight you? There're plenty more reivers where Vane came from. And they won't stop because you're a fledgling. Or give a damn that you're part of the clan. They're out to get what they want, no matter what."

* * *

Beck was breathing hard, more out of the sexual hormones spiking in her system than because she actually needed the oxygen. She lifted her hips hard trying to dislodge him. No response. Nothing. Nada. Well, that was if she didn't count the rock hard erection she'd definitely felt. Even with her newly found vampire strength, she wasn't a match for a centuries-seasoned warrior trained old school. But she had one thing he underestimated—pure twenty-first-century spunk.

She watched his mouth as he spoke, wanting desperately to kiss him. But he'd made it plain he was only her mentor. The council had made it plain that an imprint between them was unacceptable. Kissing him would only make her want more. Things he couldn't give her.

He looked down at her, his face reserved except for his eyes, which smoldered with longing. "You can't leverage me off you. Use what you have."

"You've got my hands pinned. What do want me to do?" she asked with sarcasm. If she did reach up and kiss him, that would certainly throw him off balance. God knew it had the last time she'd done it.

"What would you do if I were Vane?"

"That blond red-eyed jerk?" All thoughts of kissing fled.

Achilles nodded.

Flick. Her razor sharp fangs descended and she whipped her head to the side to tear at his wrist with her mouth. He simply moved his hand and hers out of her range as if he'd anticipated the move.

"Good basic reaction, but you're forgetting something. You're a woman. You've got more muscle in your legs and hips than a man. Use it. Wrap your legs around me. Squeeze hard."

She complied, bringing her thighs up and around him, pressing in against his hips, her calves and heels digging into his butt, pushing him right against her hot, wet heat. Let him bite on *that*.

"Good." The edge of his voice wavered.

Sheer power radiated through her, making her skin tingle. *Not as tough as you look, are you?* Sure, it had started as merely a training exercise, but having her legs wrapped around his waist brought her far too close for him to remain the stoic warrior.

"If you squeeze hard enough you can pinch nerves in the spine." Her hold on him softened, her thighs becoming more pliable rather than rigid against him.

Something shifted in the air around them. Beck saw the change in him, and an instant later, a buzz started in the back of her brain, an insatiable need, primitive and primal. He rolled them both, bringing her up to straddle him. Beck settled her weight on him letting the hard length of him press against her aching core. "So do vampires usually give up that easily in hand-to-hand combat?" She gave a slow roll of her hips. He growled low and deep. A feral sound that ratcheted up her own need.

"You forget yourself, fledgling." His voice betrayed that his control was frayed at the edges.

She leaned down putting one hand on either side of

his head, the sensitive tips of her breasts brushing against his bare chest, as she stared into his face. His eyes had darkened to emerald and his firm, sensual lips parted. Just below his upper lip peeked the tips of his fangs. She leaned in closer.

"You know you want me," she taunted. "I know I want you. We're both adults. Both vampires. Besides…" She reached forward, stroking his right fang lightly with the tip of her finger. Beck felt a half groan, half growl rumble deep from his belly beneath her thighs. The sound shimmered through her and torqued her own need up another notch. "Your fangs are already showing."

"You have no idea what you're doing to me."

"Then show me."

He grasped her head firmly in his hands and brought her mouth within kissing distance. She closed her eyes, waiting. But instead of his lips, the tip of his warm tongue curved over her upper lip and slowly and deliberately laved one of her fangs in a smooth downward stroke. Beck felt the brush of it all the way through to her core, as if he had stroked her intimately with his tongue. She shivered and gasped, her body quivering, already at the edge of her control. Her eyes opened wide. "Oh. My. God."

"Told you." His husky voice vibrated him against her making the ache worse, the need more intense.

"Yes, but you didn't say I'd feel it there!" She ground her mons against him to prove her point.

Achilles hissed, fangs fully bared now, eyes so green

they glowed. "We must stop this, woman. Now is not the time, nor the place. And this is not a game."

"But I know you want to play." She writhed against him, teetering on the edge of pleasure so acute it was painful. "Achilles. *Please.*"

He brushed his fingertips gently over her eyelids. "Close your eyes."

She did.

And he vanished.

She felt the rush of air and the dissipation of heat the instant he left. Her eyes snapped open and she glared around the gym.

Where are you?

Where I can keep from harming either of us. Trust me.

Beck had no idea where Achilles had gone. Her chest ached and tightened, the pleasant heat leaving her limbs.

Suddenly she felt the glide of his warm palm against the base of her spine. A shiver of delight radiating outward to every nerve ending.

Where are you? She reached out with her mind trying to find him.

It doesn't matter, wherever you are, I'm there with you. The warmth of his body was palpable, brushing against her as if he held her in his arms. No matter that she couldn't see him, she could feel him, truly feel him. The warm solidity of his chest, the strength of his arms. His hand cupped her cheek and his mouth pressed against hers, coaxing and tasting her.

You always taste like cherries.

Her nape tingled with the pressure and damp warmth of his lips kissing a trail from her mouth along her jaw. His heated breath tickled the shell of her ear.

Time for lesson six. Vampires can make love with the mind.

Shouldn't that be lesson sex?

His husky laugh was followed by the sensation of fingers trailing languidly from her shoulder, down the sensitive inner bend of her elbow to her hand. His large, strong fingers closed around hers, giving them a squeeze as he kissed her.

Beck stared at her hand. He was there, yet he wasn't. Her scientific mind said it wasn't possible.

How does it work?

Stopping worrying about why and just trust me.

The word trust went down with a hard swallow. Beck closed her eyes and groaned as her invisible lover pressed a kiss at the sensitive juncture of her neck and shoulder. Along her neck. Down between her breasts and across her stomach, all at the same time. *Why does it feel like you've got three mouths?*

He chuckled. *You need to realize, sweetling, the mind is infinite. Vampire sex isn't like human sex. I can do as much as you like, wherever you like, no waiting required.*

To underscore his wild assertion, she suddenly felt the warmth of his hand brush against her breasts, fingers and a warm mouth drawing her nipples into tight exquisitely sensitive peaks. At the same moment his hands kneaded her bottom, his fingers skimming along the cleft, and stroking her intimately. Yet another set of tender hands undid her ponytail, running through her hair and massaging her scalp, as a damp line of kisses trailed over each individual rib. Already swollen with need, and damp, Beck flexed her thighs together to stem the ache.

You see? he whispered, the words tickling in her ear.

Beck writhed on the mat, almost out of her mind with need. She reached forward. If he could do this to her, surely she could do the same to him. She was a vampire after all, wasn't she?

She imagined the rippled plane of his stomach and pictured her fingers tracing the fine golden arrow of hair below his waist.

Achilles growled. *You learn quickly, sweetling.*

Beck pictured his firm mouth beneath hers, her tongue sliding slowly, twirling around first one of his fangs and then the other as her fingers closed around his shaft.

Time and space shifted and she felt him shudder, his groan rippling through her. She arched her back off the mat.

Achilles. Where are you? I need to feel—

But before she could even complete the thought he was somehow there. Stretching her, filling her with the heated hard length of him. But there was more, so much more than just the fierce fullness and the delicious friction of him sliding against her. Beck reached down and felt only wet shorts and underwear, but by God he was there.

It's real, sweetling. The tension and heat radiating off him soaked through her clothes as if there were no barrier between them, only naked, glorious skin, silk over steel.

Where are you? she screamed in her head. Suddenly the ache spiraled out of control. Somehow she felt him too, as he lost control and came undone. The strain of his body against hers was as real as anything she'd ever felt before.

With you. I am always with you.

The air shifted as he brushed a kiss to her temple and against her cheek before firmly taking her mouth in a sweet, drugging kiss. Then he was gone.

Out in the parking garage of the complex, behind the dark tint of the Bugatti Veyron's windows, Achilles lay his head back against the head cushion of his seat and thought he might expire. He was spent, well and truly spent.

He cursed in Greek, Latin and English.

There was only so much a man could resist.

Achilles closed his eyes and beat himself softly on the forehead with the round of his fist. "You. Dumb. Idiot."

Suddenly the locks on the doors of the Veyron clicked open and his car door whipped open. Achilles had no chance to react before Vane pulled him from his seat and slammed his ass up against the side of his car.

"For once I agree with you." Vane's platinum spiked hair glowed almost white beneath the lights of the parking garage, his skin looking ghostly next to the black leather duster he wore.

How had Vane penetrated their outer defenses? It wasn't something he could have accomplished on his own. "What the hell are you doing here?"

His pale lip curled into a sneer over a lethal smile, fangs glinting. "Someone would like a little word with you." Vane's red eyes glowed with pure delight and malice as they transported from the garage.

Chapter 11

The streets of New York were busy in the growing twilight, the honking horns and shush of tires on pavement close by. But rather than in the streets, they landed in a filthy, malodorous side alley that housed overflowing trash containers.

Vanc's black leather duster swirled around their feet as they materialized from transporting. He opened his hands, dropping fistfuls of Achilles's shirt, then stepped away, hands raised.

"Next time," Achilles drawled, as he, too, stepped back, smoothing out the wrinkles in his shirt where Vane had grabbed hold of him. "*Ask before you touch me.* I don't give a rat's ass *who* the hell you think you are. I won't be summoned like a serf. I'll break your hands the next time you touch me."

What he wouldn't give for a nice sharp broadsword right about. But Vane was only one reiver. The bigger problem was whoever had helped Vane get inside the clan complex as a messenger boy. If Vane could get that close, then Vane could get to Rebecca. And Achilles wasn't about to let that happen.

"You'd best mind your manners, vampire, if you want to keep that pretty head on your shoulders," Vane taunted.

Achilles glanced around, tense, waiting for reivers to attack. "Who else is on the guest list? It's hardly going to be a party with just two of us bloodied up."

Vane turned, glancing over his shoulder, and lifted the corner of his lip in a perfect punk rocker sneer. "You'll see."

The slow hum of tires on pavement caused Achilles to scan the dark tunnel of the alley. A white stretch limo blocked that exit. There were other ways and means to leave, but he was curious. He wanted to know who or what had wormed into the clan complex's outer perimeter without setting off the alarms. If he were lucky and survived, perhaps Vane would inadvertently answer some of the questions Achilles had.

The door of the limo opened and shut, but he could see no one approaching. Whoever they were, they were ancient enough to cloak themselves from view. Powerful enough to outwit the charms and protections around the outer rim of the clan complex.

The scent alone indicated rogue vampire. But also something more.

Something worse.

From the prickle on his neck Achilles knew the vampire or vampires approaching had less than the best of intentions.

Oh, now, that's harsh, a familiar female voice purred.

A black mist curled along the edges of the alley, filling the floor with a dark fog that smelled suffocatingly sweet like lilies. Only one being caused chaos for her pleasure.

Eris?

Hello, Achilles. Long time no fight.

A harsh gust of wind tugged at his hair, and scraped his face. Papers and leaves pitched and twirled down the street in uneasy cartwheels. The swirl of black mist eddied in the agitated air before him, knitting quickly into the form of a woman. A beautiful woman, incongruously dressed in a pearl gray suit jacket that draped in soft artful falls from her shoulders and matching pencil skirt that clung to her thighs.

The ends of her honey blond hair swayed against the tops of her petite shoulders, and several strands of perfect pearls looped along her graceful throat. Wispy bangs swept over the pale sweet oval of her face half hiding a pair of guileless clear blue eyes. Her generous pale pink, highly glossed lips curved into a sensuous smile. But he knew from hard-won experience that looks could be deceiving.

Eris, daughter of Ares, god of war, was only interested in one thing: chaos. Inspiring conflicting emotions was her specialty. Achilles tamped down the metallic bite of fear surging in the back of his throat. She was a hell of a lot more to fear than Vane ever could be.

Eris fed upon war, fear, anxiety, pain and arguments as surely as vampires fed on blood.

"I've missed you," she said, the saccharine tone barely covering her malicious intent.

A bone deep chill swept through him. Being the focus of her attention was never a good thing. "What the hell do you want?"

Her eyes sparkled as if he'd just offered her a deep rich dark chocolate. "Can't I have a visit with my *favorite* vampire now and then?"

Damn. He had to have better control. "No."

She narrowed the gap between them and drew a French-manicured nail along his jaw. The nail transformed midstroke to a black talon. The sharp point leaving a thin stinging cut along his jaw. "Since we've no time at present for more interesting games, I shall be woefully brief. I'm taking your fledgling."

His gut coiled. *Not Rebecca.* Showing anger or fear would only feed her need for it. He opted for a casual monotone. "What do you want with her?"

"I can't have her interrupting my delicious plans. Besides, Vane was very put out that you took his fledgling to mentor without even asking. He so enjoyed her mother."

Achilles glanced behind him at Vane. He lounged up against the grimy bricks, one booted foot behind him. He swiped his reddish tongue over one fang.

Achilles fought back a surge of anger. "Taking her

won't stop the clan. They will level the laboratory and stop the creation of the vaccine because they think it will be used to kill vampires."

"Oh, it will. I've seen to that." Her confirmation numbed him like a plunge in an icy river. It sucked away his ability to think, to act. By sheer will alone, Achilles fought back the dark power Eris cast around her.

He looked at her with a steady, level gaze. "Vanquish will not be allowed to remain in the hands of mortals. My clan and the others will stop it, and you."

She closed her sparkling eyes, sniffing the putrid air with appreciation. "Wonderful." She cast her gaze on him, a smile curling her pink glossy lips, and tipped her head to the side. "I don't really care who suffers in the process as long as *someone* does."

"Always hungry, aren't you?" he asked.

"A goddess has to eat. My favorite warrior isn't going to disappoint me, is he?"

He shrugged. "I'm afraid I have no option. It isn't my call how they handle the situation. I'll, of course, encourage the clan to seek a peaceful resolution."

She leaned in, her wintergreen-scented breath causing a chill to skate over his skin. "Careful vampire. If you cross me, I'll take matters into my own hands. The clan will discover how truly instrumental you were in my release back into the world."

For over almost two thousand years she'd been locked up in a special cage, created from silver and orichalcum that was located underneath the Greek Parthenon, just waiting to be set free. And just as the twentieth century had dawned, she had been released by the brothers of the Sang Noir Guild—the secret vampire military he'd been part of since its inception.

Without the goddess the imbalance had become too great. In the vacuum humanity had turned to destroying themselves. Restoring Eris to her rightful place had led to world wars and natural disasters, but it had also restored balance as people formed alliances and became heroes and gave humanity a chance to survive. It was a choice he and the other members of the Sang Noir Guild were forced to make for the benefit of all. Without humanity, there would be no new vampires. Without humanity, vampires would someday cease to exist.

But after so many centuries of being denied her just due, Eris had been ravenous. Two world wars and a host of cataclysmic volcanoes, earthquakes, floods and hurricanes, her personal favorite, hadn't been enough. Achilles knew, even as his gut formed a Gordian Knot around the problem, that World War III was just waiting around the corner. And he bore responsibility for setting her free.

If the council, or even Dmitri, ever discovered his role in Eris's release, he'd be beheaded, as would the other members of the guild if they were revealed. And an imprinted Rebecca, if she wasn't already returned to mortal, would suffer.

Achilles forced a leisurely smile. "Whatever works for you, babe."

Bluc lightning flashed behind Eris's eyes. Her glossed

lips pressed into a teeth-baring snarl, the ends of her hair writhing like snakes. "You cannot deny me my due, vampire. No one can," she snapped.

He held up his hands. "When you're right, you're right, goddess."

"Insufferable vampire." She spun away, her pale gray jacket rippling and turning on the spot into black mist as she vaporized.

He glanced over to discover Vane had disappeared as well. Thank the gods for small favors.

Achilles transported back to Seattle, where he'd left Rebecca safe inside the Cascade Clan's complex. At least Eris couldn't touch her there. Beyond the sheer number of powerful vampires who lived there, the complex was protected by enchantments and blood magic. Older magic that even Eris had to respect or face the wrath of the other gods.

Achilles found Rebecca in the atrium, her wet hair spiraling in damp dark curls around her shoulders. Clothed in a pair of blue jeans that hugged her derriere, and a black hooded sweatshirt that hid her other assets. He placed a hand on her shoulder and she started, whipping around to face him.

Her eyes widened, then narrowed, as she held a small package pressed against her chest.

"I should have known," she muttered and started stalking away from him in the direction of the exit to the parking garage elevator.

"Miss me?"

She threw a hard glare at him. "Do you know how stupid I felt laying there by myself when Kris walked in and thought I was having some kind of fit?"

At least she'd been safe. Pure fear sliced into him as he thought of what would have happened had Vane been able to take them both. "Sorry. I had no choice."

"Really." The sarcastic edge to her voice came through loud and clear. "Because if that's how it works, count me out. I'm not interested in a repeat performance."

He moved quickly, catching up in a few long strides. "I had a security matter to attend to."

Her steps faltered a moment as she slowed and turned to face him. The sheepish look on her face was priceless. "I'm sorry. I'm probably overreacting, aren't I?"

He slipped a finger beneath her chin and tipped up her face so he could look deeply into her eyes. "I've been a vampire for millennia, Rebecca. There is nothing you could do or say that I haven't already endured. You can't hurt me, so don't worry about it. I'm the one supposed to be protecting you. Got it?"

· She nodded, but nibbled at her lip. "I just never have had very good luck at this sort of thing. Usually I end up scaring guys away because I'm too standoffish or too pushy. Either way I can't seem to get it right."

"That was before you became a vampire."

"Yes, but I'm not going to stay one."

His jaw tightened. That was the plan, wasn't it? "Yes, but once you've been a vampire, you can never go back to being just another mortal. Men will find you utterly irresistible."

Rebecca wove her fingers into the end of her damp hair, twining the dark strands around her white fingers. Light and dark, two halves of the same whole. Sure, he wanted her to realize they already shared something she'd never have with another being on this planet. The imprint was real enough between him and Ione. Despite her being reborn, it was still real. Only Rebecca didn't have memories of her life before. Did she?

"Have you ever wanted to go to Greece?" The question seemed random enough.

She squinted her eyes for a second, a small half smile lifting part of her kissable lips. "Yeah. I've always dreamed of traveling there someday."

"And what makes you interested in it?"

"I don't know, I just have this feeling that I'm missing something, something that I'd find there. And I've had dreams about aquamarine clear water and a patch of endless blue cloudless sky seen through tall white columns."

Memories of her life as Ione, he'd bet his left fang on it. But pushing her to remember would only strengthen the imprint.

I need her to go back to being mortal as soon as possible so this damn imprint will end.

As if responding to his thought, the package in her hand slipped and tumbled from her fingers. He caught it before it hit the floor and handed it back to her, gazing deeply into her eyes.

"Thank you. I'm glad you caught that. It might have broken."

"What's in it?"

"The ichor sample Eva left me."

And if Eris had her way, the key to the suffering of millions, human and vampire, Achilles thought as he phased the keys to the Veyron into his hand and gripped them tight.

As much as he would like to protect them all, right now his duty was to protect and instruct Rebecca—and to find a way to grant her desire to return to being human.

"What do you need to test it?"

"A superfund and unlimited time?"

"Very funny, Doc, but unfortunately we're not dealing with a humorous situation. Things just got a lot more complicated. What would be the ETA on getting this ichor substituted in your current frankenvirus creation?"

Rebecca shoved her drying hair out of her face. "Starting from scratch, I'm looking at three months minimum."

Achilles thought about the imprint. Hell, he'd be lucky if they had a week or more before it was fully formed. And every training session was solidifying it. "And if you don't start from scratch?"

"If I can get the first version of the vaccine, I can do a PCR substitution. Rough estimate one week to know if its viable, but that would be pushing it."

A sucking pull started just behind his navel and

Achilles grabbed hold of Rebecca's waist. He knew he was being transported and was afraid what might happen if he left her behind. "Hang on, sweetling, we're going for a ride."

Chapter 12

When they arrived in Dmitri's office, Beck was gasping for breath. She pressed a hand to the center of her twisting stomach. "What was that?"

"Transporting. Sorry, wasn't like I had much time to explain it to you." He glanced at Dmitri. "Nice of you to warn me first."

Dmitri's left brow rose, a glimmer of wariness flashing in his dark eyes. "I didn't expect her to be with you."

Achilles remained stoic. "We've been working on basics."

"And she still hasn't mastered transport yet?"

"I don't think it's the teacher," Beck said. She thought it was only fair that Dmitri know the lessons hadn't been poorly done, they'd just been—well, intense.

Dmitri shifted in his chair, brushing his lip with an index finger. "Are you proving a difficult fledgling?"

Beck stiffened.

Dmitri cleared his throat. "I've heard an absolutely absurd rumor and I need to quash it."

Achilles crossed his arms, the package of ichor disappearing from his hand, as he braced his feet wide apart. "Hit me."

"I've had two members of the council come to me with reports that they may have reason to suspect you of dealings with Eris." He looked meaningfully at Achilles, his chin tilted down, his dark brows drawn together. "Tell me, brother, that this is some sick reiver jest."

The air grew heavy with tension. "I wish I could, but I've never lied to you and I'm sure as hell not going to start now."

A crushed looked flitted over Dmitri's features an instant before they hardened so completely his profile appeared to be carved of granite. "What have you done?"

Achilles pulled back his shoulders, seeming to grow larger, and widened his stance like a warrior. "Nothing you wouldn't have done in my place. After two thousand years, the Sang Noir Guild decided that it was time to release her."

"The Guild decided to let the goddess of chaos loose on the world? What in the name of all that's holy were you thinking?"

"The intention was to feed her and put her back, not let her loose."

Dmitri glared at him. "The path to chaos is littered with good intentions."

Achilles shook his head. "You weren't there when the Guild decided. Holding her captive like that just didn't seem right."

"How in the hell can holding the goddess of chaos captive seem wrong?" Beck blurted.

Achilles turned to her, his eyes blazing green. "Is it right to punish something for its very nature? Would you lock away a bird because it flies or kill a cat because it hunts, or behead a vampire because it craves blood? No. It is the very nature of the thing. Civility may bend our natures, shape them to what is acceptable, but underneath lies fallow the true heart of things. Nature cannot be denied indefinitely. Just as there is light in the world so there must be darkness to balance it. The other elite warriors with me in the Guild believed we were doing what was best to save the world."

"Is this whole philosophy lesson going anywhere, professor, because as far as I can tell this Eris chick is seriously bad news," Beck interjected.

Annoyance and anger filled the air with the scent of acrid smoke and pepper, and it was coming from Achilles's direction. For a second Beck sniffed the air again just to be sure. Her vampire senses were still new enough to her that she wasn't sure what was normal for a vampire and what wasn't. But Achilles couldn't be serious. Balance was one thing, every scientist knew that, but chaos?

"We needed her."

"Then you've got a lot more problems than merely shutting down the vampire vaccine production." Dmitri's fingers wove together into a tight knot.

Achilles grunted.

"Shut it down! You never said anything about shutting it down." Beck's gaze darted from one mountain-size man to the other. She wanted to knock both their heads together. Did they even have a clue how much work was invested in that vaccine?

The look in Achilles's eyes begged her to shut up, but Beck wasn't in the mood to listen. "Look, I'm going to find a way to go back to being a damn mortal even if I have to start from scratch."

"You'll get your chance before we shut down the operation," he assured her, shooting a meaningful look at Dmitri.

"You can't just shut it down, it's a virus," Beck spluttered.

"And we've got reason to believe your precious investors are planning on using it as a biological weapon against our kind," Achilles fired back. "So what would you have me do, Rebecca? Stand aside and let those I've sworn to protect be put in danger, or take action?"

Beck nibbled at her lip. Of course he was going to take action. A man like Achilles didn't know what a sideline was let alone how to stay there.

"But I swear to you, you will get a chance to become mortal before we shut it down."

"Then I need at least a month."

Achilles looked at Dmitri. Dmitri glared hard at

Achilles. "Don't push your luck, brother. As *Trejan* I have only so much leeway with you before my head goes on the block, as well. We move when the council orders it."

"I appreciate you standing by me all the same."

Dmitri gave a gruff nod. "I will do all I can for you and your fledgling." Behind them the door opened all on its own.

Beck suspected it was Dmitri using some vampire power she'd yet to hear of. Obviously it was time to go. Beck turned on her heel and walked through the door and kept going, her mind spinning the entire time. Getting into Genet-X without clearance was nearly impossible. She glanced at Achilles's Rolex—7:00 p.m. wasn't late enough. Most of the lab regulars would be gone, but certainly not Margo if she was working overtime. By 10:00 p.m. the night security staff would be in place. It would still be risky, but possible.

"So where did the package go?" Beck asked.

"Package?"

"Eva's ichor. I saw you phase it."

"You wanted it sent to Margo, didn't you?"

"Yeah."

He nodded. "It should be sitting on her desk."

"So what's the plan?" Beck asked.

Achilles eyed her as they walked shoulder to shoulder down the hall. "You still need a sample of the initial vaccine to work with the new ichor, don't you?"

She nodded. "Starting with what we've already got would save me months of work."

"Then we're going to need to get access to it, if not by regular means, then by stealth."

Beck came to a complete halt. "Whoa. Hold up. I am not some kind of vampire warrior on a mission here. That's you. I'm a scientist who wants to go back to the way I was originally."

"Since we don't know exactly what to be prepared for, it would be best if you learned the trifecta of vampire moves. Just to be on the safe side."

"Which is?"

"Phasing, transporting and becoming invisible. The last I wouldn't teach a fledgling this early, but under the circumstances I don't see another option."

Beck cocked her hip and folded her arms. "So, what's up first, professor?"

"Have you been able to phase anything?" Achilles cracked his neck to the side and rolled his shoulders.

Beck shook her head wondering just how strenuous it was going to be. "I've tried, but either I'm not concentrating enough or I'm not doing it right."

"Show me."

She screwed her eyes shut and thought about a glass of lemonade appearing in her outstretched hand. The smooth glass was frosted, cold to the touch, the pale yellow transparent liquid sweet and tart, making the back of her mouth ache with the lemony scent. Her hand dipped with the weight of something in her palm, but it definitely wasn't a smooth glass. She cracked open one eye to find a lemon in her hand.

Beck sighed, gripping the lemon and shaking it. "See what I mean? Close but not exactly."

"You aren't focusing on the total experience, just the last part of it." Achilles stepped closer to her, pulling the lemon out of her hand and pitching it up into the air where it vanished. His large hand closed firmly around hers making it seem small in comparison. He tugged her hand, twirling her into the circle of his arms, her back against his chest.

"Let's try it again. This time I want you to think of a glass of champagne. Not just drinking it, or the taste, but the whole experience, the essence of champagne. How it makes you feel." He skipped his fingers upward from her wrists to her shoulders, like the rising bubbles in a glass. She shivered. "Good. Now close your eyes."

Beck complied, her lids fluttering shut, the warmth of him radiating against her back. How had she ever thought he felt cold? He was as hot as they came, and then some. He pressed still closer, his arm brushing against the length of hers as he held her hand.

Focus. Champagne, dry taste, bubbles. She inhaled deeply, trying to concentrate on the feeling sparkling deep down in her solar plexus, now radiating from her shoulder to her hand.

"Let those sensations fill you up, become solid form, hold it, own it," he whispered, his words searing her ear and making the small hairs on her skin raise in attention. "Good, I can feel it in you. Now call it to you, and expect it to materialize."

The weight was cool and heavy, the glass smooth

and dry beneath her fingers. Beck opened both eyes in surprise and stared at the glass of champagne in her hand. "I did it," she breathed.

Achilles stepped back from her. "Yes, you did." The cool rush of air between them triggered an ache in her chest. She missed the feeling of him next to her. Ached for it more than she did air.

She turned, looking up into his face, beautiful, but masculine and just rough enough to send a message he wasn't someone to be messed with. But his eyes as he stared at her were a weird mixture of tenderness and wariness. "We should move on." The glass of champagne evaporated as if it had never been.

She swallowed hard against the ache creeping up her throat. As much as she wanted to learn what he had to teach her, it also made her sad. Each sensation, each experience, would only be memories. Each one brought her closer to being away from him forever.

You're a scientist. Learn what you can from it, then move on, she reminded herself. She straightened her shoulders and lifted her chin. Sheesh. No one had told her that fine line of love cut like a razor blade. It hurt. She shook her head to clear it.

No, not love. She was in lust with him. Who wouldn't be? Sexual chemistry. Purely chemical. Purely an autonomic body response she had no logical control of. But it wasn't love.

"I think the next thing we are going to work on is transporting." He tore his gaze away from her, but not before she caught a glimpse of the fleeting wounded look in his eyes. Achilles cleared his throat, then huffed out a breath. When he leveled his gaze at her once again, he was back to stoic warrior, and Beck wondered if she'd merely imagined the emotion in him.

"Transporting is an extension of phasing," he said evenly, as if they'd never touched. Never kissed. Never made love in a whole different way than she ever had before. "However, instead of bringing the object to you, you are taking yourself to the person, place or thing. Got it?"

"Sort of."

He grasped her shoulders gently. His deep green eyes were serene, deep, reassuring. "You can do this, sweetling." He slid one hand down placing it over the flat of her stomach. The muscles there tightened and her tummy flipped in response to his touch. Worse, the insistent throbbing at the juncture of her thighs distracted her from what Achilles was saying. "Sorry. Repeat that."

"When you concentrate on a location, imagine yourself appearing there. Think about what you'll see, and hear. The way the air will taste. You'll feel a pull behind your navel. That will mean you've begun to move. The important thing is to concentrate on your destination. If you lose focus you could end up somewhere you never intended, or not move at all."

"Focus. Right." How was she supposed to focus when he was still touching her? "But what if I've never been there, can I transport there?"

The shake of his head was almost imperceptible. "No,

not unless you've got a phenomenal imagination. Your impression of the destination has to be crystal clear." He let go of her and Beck immediately felt the loss, as if the warmth of the sun had suddenly been shielded by clouds.

"Go ahead. Pick somewhere within the clan complex for your first transport."

Beck closed her eyes, picturing the light translucent planes of glass and the white furniture of the atrium. She could hear the burbling sound of the waterfall and smell the plants. Suddenly it felt as if someone had looped a rope around her waist and was pulling her backward. Beck gasped at the sensation. The air smelled different and the sound of water running wasn't just in her imagination.

She opened her eyes and found herself in the atrium. A second later Achilles transported in beside her.

Beck bounced on her toes, clasping her hands together, a ridiculously giddy feeling of pride bubbling up in her chest. "I did it. I did it! I can transport!"

Achilles's full-on smile lit up the entire atrium, stealing her ability to think. "Well done."

"And I can take myself anywhere like this?"

"Anywhere you've been before."

Beck closed her eyes and thought of her own cozy home. Specifically her bedroom. The big pinks and lavenders of the cabbage roses on her bedspread seemed far less inviting than she had imagined. She hadn't told him where she was going on purpose. For a moment she needed some space away from those broad shoulders and killer smiles. She waited a moment, then one more, just to be sure Achilles wasn't going to follow her.

Like hell, Achilles thought as he watched her from the corner of her room, invisible to her, and listening in on her thoughts. He wasn't letting her go anywhere without knowing exactly who was there and what was happening.

She glanced around, sighed, then pulled the black hooded sweatshirt over her head and peeled off her T-shirt.

Rebecca shucked out of her jeans, letting them shimmy down over the curve of her hips and down her lean legs. All she was wearing underneath was a little black scrap of nothing they called a G-string. Curious. Perhaps there was even more to her than he'd imagined.

All it did was make the ache more intense. Every fiber of him ached.

Her pale skin brought out the red highlights in her chestnut curls, the ones above and the ones peeping out below. He couldn't stop the low rumble in his chest.

The imprint flared to life vicious in its intensity. He was already hard.

Rebecca whipped around, covering her near perfect breasts with her arms. Protective, but utterly useless as it only enhanced her cleavage more.

"Achilles?" she whispered harshly, her narrowed gaze darting around the room.

He fluxed, releasing his invisibility, and her eyes burned with fury.

"How long have you been there?"

"Long enough to know I need to tell you something."

She lifted her chin. "Then tell me and get out."

He crossed the room so quickly, she barely had time to suck in a startled breath. Fighting the imprint was becoming useless.

He pulled her into his arms. "You smell fantastic." The scent of her was so addictive he couldn't seem to get enough of it. He inhaled, letting it fill him up and bent his head, nuzzling along her neck.

Her breath hitched. "You, you wanted to tell me that?"

"No." Her skin was like hot silk beneath his lips as he kissed a path to her lush mouth.

"What, wha—what did you want to tell me?"

He pulled back long enough to look into her eyes, to lose himself in the hazy, heated longing he saw there. Gods, she was as affected by the imprint as he was. He could tell it from the way she looked, the way she smelled, the jasmine scent of vampire attraction growing more intense. And then there had been her thoughts. She actually believed she was falling in love with him. Aw hell. It was only the imprint. She just didn't know that, yet.

Achilles pulled her closer, reveling in the feel of her bare skin beneath his hands.

"I want you." He crushed his mouth to hers in a kiss both demanding and pleading.

A soft yielding moan echoed in her throat, vibrating

straight through him. She wrapped her arms around his neck, pulling him closer, pressing and rasping her barely covered breasts against his chest. He deepened the kiss, letting the sunshine of her wash over him. Her light wiped out the darkness within him. She fairly glowed with it.

She wrapped herself around him like a vine, her leg twining about his, her fingers tangling in fistfuls of his shirt. One moment he was rock steady absorbing everything she offered, the next he was falling. She'd pressed herself into him, purposely throwing them both off balance so that they landed on the bed. His fingers explored the curve of her spine and she shivered beneath his touch.

Her lips buzzed against his as she purred with satisfaction, her soft, devilishly clever tongue stroking his. Her fingers dug into his shirt, ripping it to shreds. She stopped kissing him for a moment and glanced down at the mess she'd made of the fabric. "Sorry. Guess I still don't know my own strength."

"Don't care. Have others. There's only one you."

Her slightly kiss-swollen lips curved into a smile that made his body throb. "Show me." Her husky whisper against his mouth nearly vaulted him off the mattress. He could have damn well levitated with the force of his reaction to her.

The phone rang, sharp and insistent on her nightstand. "Let it go to voice mail," he growled.

The machine she used to screen calls beeped in the

next room, a woman's voice coming through loud and clear. "Hey, Beck. It's Margo. If you're there, pick up."

Rebecca stiffened in his arms. "I've got to take that."

He nodded, brushing a kiss to her temple and felt something inside him shrivel, wilt and die. He hated to let her go. And it wasn't just this moment. He knew instinctively the call would change everything between them.

Chapter 13

Beck rolled away from him and fumbled for the phone on her nightstand, her voice echoing on the machine in the next room. "Hey, Margo. I'm here."

"I've done it! We've done it!"

"Wait, back that up a sec. Do you mean to tell me it worked?" She took the phone with her into the living room so she could turn off the answering machine.

"Yes, the new ichor you gave me worked like a charm. The new vaccine turns people back to human in forty-eight hours."

"That's great news!" She turned to see Achilles had followed and was standing in the doorway to her bedroom, his shoulder leaning against the doorjamb. He'd phased a new shirt to replace the one she'd literally ripped off of him. The air chilled her skin and she realized she was only in her bra and panties. She phased a soft cotton bathrobe for herself. Then was stunned and pleased that she'd actually done so.

"There's only one hitch."

Beck pushed the button on the recorder, shutting off the speaker. She had a really bad feeling about that one hitch. "What's that?"

"It turns them back into whatever their true chronological age is. Not so bad for those who've only been recently changed against their will like you and Kris. More problematic for people who've had long-term exposure."

Beck's stomach pitched. This was bad. Very bad. And not at all what she'd expected. "Are you telling me it kills older vampires?"

"Theoretically speaking, aging that fast would kill anything," Margo quipped as if it were humorous. "But yes. I tested it."

It wasn't funny in the least to Beck. "It kills vampires."

"*No,* it doesn't. It only returns them to their human state."

But they were already human. Different, *but human.* She had to do something. "Wait, Margo. You can't hand that over to the investors. That's not a vaccine, that's genocide. If you let that virus out to the general public, you're going to potentially kill thousands of vampires who haven't done anything."

"So?"

Anger bubbled up inside Beck making her gum line

throb and her temperature kick up a notch. "Don't you care that you're taking innocent lives?"

Margo uttered a long-suffering sigh. "They're not alive. They're undead, remember." A heavy pause interrupted their conversation and when Margo spoke again her voice was dripping with accusation. "Wait. I see what's happening. Now that you've had to be one, you think you can play both sides. Well, here's the reality, Beck. You're either with them or you're with the rest of us humans. What's it going to be?"

Beck held back the fangs that were aching to come out, an uncomfortable mixture of anger and loyalty percolating inside her. "I want to go back to being mortal, but I don't see the reason why we have to wipe out all of them in the process. People should have a choice to be vampire or not. That's what this whole vaccine has always been about."

"Only for you. The investors want a way to keep humans safe from the vampire virus—to control or eliminate it the way we did with small pox. The vaccine works and I'm giving it to the investors."

Beck gripped the phone so tightly the hard plastic casing cracked. "Margo, please, stop and think this through—" She didn't get a chance to finish before the dial tone told her Margo wasn't interested in anything more she had to say.

"Dammit," she muttered and chucked the phone across the room where it shattered against the wall.

"I take it that your chat with Margo didn't go well."

She turned and looked Achilles in the eye. A sudden

ache, deep and pulsing, took up residence in her heart. "If Margo does what I think she's going to do, vampires are toast."

"Then we'll have to find a way to stop her."

His determination was heroic enough, but utterly asinine. You couldn't fight science, except with science.

"We can't. Vanquish isn't just a vaccine anymore. It's a vampire pesticide. Somehow Margo's manipulated whatever genetics were unique to Eva's ichor and found the key, the magic packet of DNA, that activates the aging portion of the virus."

"The plague?"

Beck nodded, her fingers catching and snaring in her curls and she shoved her hand through her hair. "It won't harm anyone who's been recently turned, just age them by a few months or at most a year or two, but for anyone who's been exposed for a long period of time..."

"They'll turn to bone dust." His voice sounded hollow.

Beck nodded again, unable to swallow past the thickness clogging her tight throat. Her eyes burned with unshed tears. Who knew that vampires could cry?

The hot tears trailed down her cheeks. Tears of regret. Tears of anger. Tears of frustration. "This is all my fault. I never should have given her Eva's ichor."

Achilles wrapped his arms around her, bringing her in close to his chest and kissing the top of her head. "You didn't know what they intended. You had only the best of intentions."

"Doesn't matter. Now all vampires are at risk. Kris. Dmitri. My mom." She pulled back looking up into his strong face. "You."

He kissed her fiercely. And when he pulled back slowly, his eyes tender, Beck was certain she never wanted to be anywhere else. How could she have been so blind to trust Margo, to truly believe that the vaccine was the answer?

"Oh, God. What are we going to do?"

He rubbed his hand over her back in a slow, soothing circle. "First, we're going to get a sample of Vanquish, then you're going to get your sweet ass into the lab and find out what scientific hoodoo Margo's performed and see if we can't create an antidote."

"That's a good plan. But I meant what are we going to do about us?"

"Us?" His eyes widened a fraction. The question had been unexpected. He'd really thought that her reverting back to being mortal was just going to make all of this imprint stuff between them float away. Men really were dense. She didn't even know exactly what an imprint was or how it worked. She only knew she felt something for him that wasn't like anything she'd ever experienced for a guy before—alive or undead.

"You told me that you'd explain exactly what an imprint was when I was further along in my training. That it didn't matter once I was mortal again because it would magically disappear. I want to go into this plan with my eyes open. What is an imprint and why were the council members willing to excommunicate you for it?"

Achilles blew out a rattling breath. The weight of his worry and loss pressed upon her shoulders like a physical thing.

"Why does it make you so sad?" she asked, her voice far smaller, far quieter than it had been.

He closed his eyes for a moment, trying to find the words he needed, then grasped her small hands folding them into his, cradling them. So fragile. Even now, as a vampire. His chest ached.

"That three-circle symbol in the council chambers stands for more than just what everyone thinks it does. Dmitri would tell you one circle is for life, another for death and the third for vampire, straddling the two— undeath. But it's more than that. It's an ancient reminder of the imprint where two vampires are interlinked as one united being. An imprint is like nothing else in the human realm. It is stronger than bonding with a mate. It is stronger than the link between a fledgling and maker. Between vampires it is enduring, and once fully formed and sealed, unbreakable."

"Until death." She said it with such certainty because she'd never known it could be any different. He gazed up at her worried expression.

He shook his head. "An imprint lasts beyond death. Slain vampires often are reborn, drawn to be made again."

"Wait, are you telling me vampires are reincarnated?"

She rolled her eyes. "Okay, professor, now I know you've gone off the deep end."

He stroked his thumb over the smooth silk of her hand, a rush of sparks entering his blood at the touch. That didn't happen every day. That was the power of an imprint at work.

"An imprint is more powerful than any one vampire."

"What exactly does that mean? We're going to share a brain or something?"

He cocked his mouth in a partial grin at her simplistic half truth. "Better…and worse. Vampires who share an imprint share their powers. They have a tighter link to each other's thoughts."

Her eyes widened enough that the green rim around the edge threatened to take over the brown clustered around the center. She squeezed his hand. "That's why I could hear Dmitri talking to you, wasn't it?"

He nodded. "Usually it takes a new vampire decades to develop that skill, even longer to develop others. You already have begun to tap into your link to my powers without even knowing how."

She lifted a brow, her hand sliding from his. "So far I'm not seeing a downside here."

He swallowed hard. Somehow the words themselves were bitter. "Vampires with an imprint also share each other's pain."

"You mean if you get hit in a fight, then I bruise?"

"Vampires don't bruise."

"Yeah, guess that would require blood, wouldn't it."

"A cut on me won't leave a mark on you, but you'd feel it just the same, just as deep."

Her face filled with a knowing look. "That's why you're so worried about it, isn't it? You don't want me to get hurt, so you think an imprint will take you out of the action. You won't be able to risk fighting anymore."

The thought had crossed his mind, but had been quickly overshadowed by something he feared far more. "No, I'm worried about what would happen to you if I'm beheaded. If I'm excommunicated and beheaded while you're still a vampire, half of you would die. Living as a halfling is a horrible existence. You can't love, you can't hope. You can't live. You merely exist."

Her face softened, the light in her eyes growing distant, colder. "Have you imprinted before?"

"Yes."

She lifted her chin and pulled her hand from his grasp. "Then how can you possibly imprint with me if it's a forever thing?"

He stared at her, concerned with how she would react to the truth.

Because it is you. You as Ione.

Fine lines of surprise creased her face and he knew she'd heard his thought.

"Oh, no. You think I'm the reincarnation of this chick you were imprinted to before?"

He stepped closer, narrowing the gap between them. "I don't think it, I know. You were Ione, and though you may not remember, the imprint never forgets. We are bound together, like it or not."

Her whole body slackened in his hands as if her strength suddenly left her. Rebecca held a hand to her head. "I suddenly don't feel so good." He gently settled her down on the couch, grabbed a pillow and placed it by her head.

"What happened to her?"

Achilles turned away unable to bear the intensity of her gaze.

"She was captured, tortured and eventually beheaded by the Inquisition."

The smell of rotting straw, sweet in comparison to the rancid odor of festering flesh and the acrid stench of burnt skin, saturated the air, making Beck gag reflexively. She glanced around and found herself surrounded by slime-covered walls of stone punctuated with shackles.

Her shoulders seared with a burning pain as did her spine, hips and knees from stretching on the rack. The skin on her bottom, newly regrown that night after having been burnt away once again on the red hot metal of the hot seat, still was too sensitive for her to sit on.

The taste of thick, cold metallic blood being poured into her mouth made Beck gasp for breath, not from the repulsive taste alone. It shot spikes of pain penetrating through her whole system, freezing her muscles and making even the movement of blinking excruciatingly painful.

"Dead man's blood. That'll keep her quiet till the monsignor is done with her." The strange voice echoed from above her.

Beck squeezed her eyes shut and shook her head,

trying to rid herself of the pure terror that had her shaking and chilled.

When she opened them again it was to find herself in Achilles's arms, his handsome face contorted into lines of pain and anxiety.

"What in the hell just happened?"

He closed his eyes and swore under his breath. "You were seeing your past. I'm sorry."

Beck tried to shrug it off, but found she couldn't. It had been too terrifying, too real, to just brush aside. She clung to him, but at the same time wanted to push away, especially if this imprint was the cause of those hideous images.

She let out a shuddering breath. "I was dying, but I couldn't die." She stared up at him, his eyes fathomless orbs of stormy green ocean.

"They fed you dead man's blood. It's a poison to vampires."

"Why was it so cold? It felt like they'd injected me with liquid nitrogen."

"There's no life force left in it. Hurts like getting hit by a eighteen-wheeler, doesn't it?"

Beck narrowed her eyes, rubbing her hand up and down her arm. The friction didn't get rid of the deep cold locked in her bones. "So were you projecting those memories into my head?"

"No. It was hard enough to live with Ione through it the first time. Why on earth would I want to experience it again?"

"So if you didn't project it, where did it come from?"

He slid his warm palm beneath the edge of her bathrobe, pressing it against her sternum. "It's part of you, wound into the strands of your DNA."

"You mean those junk strands?"

He massaged with his fingers, the warmth of them making the aching chill subside. "I don't understand how rebirth works, I only know that I've seen it in action. I know it's real. Whether you want to accept it or not, I know you were once my mentor and it ended badly."

Beck sat bolt upright, suddenly uncomfortable with being in his arms. "Look, I can't think about that right now. I don't need some five-hundred-year-old baggage on my shoulders. I've got to find a way to stop the release of Vanquish. And I don't have time for this hocus-pocus-past-life imprint stuff that you're telling me won't probably exist anymore if I turn mortal again."

Achilles released her, but the distance between them suddenly seemed far greater than just mere inches. "That's why I want you to go back to being mortal as soon as it's possible. I don't want you to suffer the way you did before."

"You mean you don't want *me* to make *you* suffer."

"That's not what I said."

"You didn't have to. Even if I couldn't read your mind, I could have read it in your eyes. You're scared. Terrified. Whatever happened between you and Ione really messed you up."

He grabbed her by the shoulders and gave her a little shake. "What happened is half of me died! I've been living as a damned halfling for five centuries. I didn't have any hope until you came back." He released her as if touching her burned him.

"What do you need to create an antivirus to Vanquish?" He sounded so resigned it made her ache, as if she'd somehow bruised him.

"I need to get a sample of what Margo's created."

"I can—"

Beck touched him. "No. You can't. If Vanquish is live and does what Margo says it can, it could react with you and you'd be dust in forty-eight hours. There's only one of us that can take that risk."

Achilles shook his head. "That doesn't mean I like it."

"You don't have to."

He lifted his head, settling his steady gaze on her. "How can I help you?"

"Tell me how to get inside the lab like a vampire."

"Unless you plan on waltzing through the lobby, then you're going to have to jump up to your lab and transport through the wall while maintaining invisibility."

"It's six freakin' stories up!"

Achilles grinned at her in a way that made her knees weak.

"Yes, but you're a vampire now. That's a workout, but not impossible."

Beck rolled her shoulders and bent her head to one side, then the other, loosening up her shoulders like an athlete.

"Okay, six stories. Jump. Got it."

"Then transport through the wall. And stay invisible."

"But we haven't even covered that yet!"

Achilles pinched the bridge of his nose. "Gods preserve me." He glanced up at her, pinning her with a sparkling green gaze. "If you'd just give me a chance, sweetling, I can teach you that, too."

He promptly disappeared and she feared the worst.

"Achilles!"

"I'm still here."

Beck noticed that rather than there being a telltale smokelike wisp, he was there one second and totally gone the next. There was nothing gradual about it. She reached out and encountered a very solid, very warm chest. Her fingers tingled.

"Just checking," she said as she worried the edge of her lip between her teeth.

An instant later he was back again, and the feeling of him beneath her touch hadn't changed.

"I'm guessing invisibility is more of an optical illusion."

"Partially. This is the part I think you'll understand better than anyone else I've trained. You're actually rearranging yourself, so that you can move through the air, become one with it. You have to mentally will yourself into nothingness."

"You mean like rearranging atoms?"

He nodded and Beck felt like a grinning fool.

"I want you to give it a try."

"Right now?" she squeaked, and pulled the lapels of her bathrobe a little tighter together.

"It's either give it a shot now and know you can, or give it a shot when you're out there on that window ledge and hope you can."

"Gotcha. Okay, here goes nothing." Beck closed her eyes, letting her mind empty.

"Very nicely done, Doc."

She popped open her eyes and held out her hand and didn't see a thing beyond the carpet and the couch and Achilles. "Thank you."

"Well, if you have no further need of me, I'm going to check back in with Dmitri and tell him of this latest development and your plans." He turned on his heel to walk away.

"Wait." A smile curved over her mouth as she tiptoed past the couch and hefted herself to sit on the counter.

He glanced over his shoulder, pinpointing exactly where she sat.

How did he know? She'd moved while she was invisible.

"Yes?"

"How do I become visible again?"

He chuckled as he strode over and stood right in front of her. "You have to focus on your body, bringing it all back together again." He stepped closer, and her knees had to part to accommodate him. "I've found wanting to do something physical usually does the trick."

Her body grew heavy and warm. "Like hit someone?"

He nodded, leaning in still closer until his mouth was only an inch away from hers. "Or kiss someone."

Beck didn't want to stop herself. She knew she was only going to be a vampire for a short while longer. So she eliminated the distance between them and threw her arms around his neck, locking him against her.

"Why don't you show me exactly how that works."

A growl rumbled low and needy in his throat. "You know we shouldn't be doing this."

"Yeah, imprint, forever, blah, blah, blah. Kiss me, already."

His lips were warm and solid and sent a shower of sparks shooting through her body, sensitizing every nerve ending. His hands curved around her ass, pulling her closer around him. With a *flick,* her fangs extended at the sensation. She saw her shoulders reappear and glanced down to see her legs wrapped around his hips. She didn't need to see his erection to feel it pressed hard against her softness.

"Mmm," she murmured against his mouth, "you still taste like black licorice."

Achilles rested his forehead against hers. "And you're killing me, Doc." With a *flick* his fangs extended as well, peering over the edge of his bottom lip.

"Then it's a good thing we're both undead." She kissed him fiercely, with everything she had, and Achilles matched the assault, making her toes curl.

Chapter 14

He pulled back long enough to stare deeply into her eyes. "You don't know how long I've been waiting for you."

"Me or the vampire I used to be?"

A valid question. He'd loved Ione with a passion, but what he felt for Rebecca ran far deeper, intertwined with his very ability to feel, to hope. She'd awakened him from a seemingly endless darkness. Achilles brushed the pad of his thumb over the incredible softness of her lip. "You."

The need to taste her, to feel her grew overwhelming. As good as he was at denial, he'd finally met his match in her. "Gods, woman." His voice was hoarse. "What am I going to do with you?"

"Easy. Make love to me. Not like a vampire, but like

the man I know you are." She closed her eyes, and he could sense the power spiraling up inside her. Without warning their clothing phased away leaving him skin to skin with her.

The sudden contact stunned him. Her wet heat pulsating against him. He ground his teeth, forcing himself to hold back from sinking deep in her. If he did this, if he surrendered to his desire for her, there'd be no going back unless she turned mortal. The imprint would be completed and his fate would be sealed, as would hers.

Deep inside, his granite heart crumbled into dust. The knowledge hit him with a force unlike anything else.

He *wanted* an imprint with her. Needed it. Even if it only lasted a short time.

Tucking her closer against him, he lost himself in the drugging power of her kiss and her touch as she kneaded his back and dug her fingernails into his skin.

He had to keep some part of her to himself forever, even if it was all he had to last him another five hundred years until she was brought back again. Someday they'd get it right, but for the moment the imprint was a pulsating, driving force that couldn't be stopped.

Slowly he traced the curves of her cheek, his fingers gliding a sensual path down her neck and over her shoulder that his mouth followed. The heat of her seared his lips as he tried to memorize every sweet inch of her fragrant skin. The soft globe of her breast created a hot silk weight in the center of his palm as he caressed it. He brushed the hardened pink tip with his thumb before drawing her into his mouth. Gods, she tasted like gingerbread, hot and spicy and sweet. Beneath his lips her nipple hardened further. Rebecca shuddered, her eyes drifting shut as she let out a soft rumbling sound from the back of her throat that torqued his response up even higher.

As he moved to taste the other side, Rebecca arched into his touch and he took everything she gave. Waking from the existence of being a halfling for so long was earth-shattering. Each touch, each caress, was magnified in intensity a hundredfold. His hand slid down the edge of her ribs and across the flare of her hip and the smooth expanse of her stomach, her skin so velvety soft it made him ache. The ichor within Rebecca moved and pulsed, the rush of it beneath her skin whispering to him like a tempting promise of redemption. Gods help him, he wanted to please her.

Rebecca panted, her breath stirring the hair on his head as she gripped his shoulders hard. He glanced up at her face. Her lush mouth was slightly open, her eyes half shuttered behind a fan of dark lashes. "Keep going," she urged. "Don't you dare stop now." The soft curls at the juncture of her thighs were damp with feminine desire as he slid his fingers into the slick cleft. Achilles trembled, drawing on everything he could to maintain his Spartan control. He'd felt her before, but that had been purely in his mind. Beneath his hands she was fire and silk. Her hips bucked toward him, pushing his touch deeper, then pulled back, allowing him to caress her.

Achilles followed her demands, his fingers stroking

her as he kissed a slow, wet path back to her mouth. Her breathing grew shallow and fast, the raw need pulsating in the air around them. Gods knew Achilles needed her—whether she was called Ione or Rebecca—in a way he'd needed no one else before or since, and he would always need her. The imprint had never diminished. It had lain dormant, waiting until he came to life once more in this woman's arms, and the drive to complete it was stronger than a mortal's need for air or a vampire's need for blood. Beck's soft, panting breath was fire against his skin.

He wished he was strong enough to deny himself for her. But Gods, no man, mortal, vampire or god was that strong. He pulled back his fingers, making her gasp with indignation, then plunged into her, making her groan. He absorbed every ounce of sensation he could. After so long separated from his other half, it was like stepping out into brilliant sunlight. Even with his eyes closed, she was pure, utter brilliance, the warmth of her soaking into every cell and bringing him back to life.

Beck threw back her head and shouted, as he pulled slowly back then slid home, filling her, completing her. But on the edges of her sexual haze, something glimmered and she instinctively knew there was something more she needed from him. He kissed a scorching trail down her neck. She arched. "Achilles," she breathed. *"Now."*

His fangs sank into her carotid, sending a bolt of electricity winding through her arteries to connect the points where they joined. Lips, breast, belly, thighs and all points in between, pulsed and throbbed as the light consumed them from the inside out.

Beck gasped. She couldn't believe the swirling intensity he brought out in her as her ichor flowed into him. It was like being a superhero, capable of seeing more, feeling more, than she'd ever imagined possible.

The sensation of him inside her was amplified a hundredfold when she realized she was experiencing not just her own überawareness of him, but of herself, as well. She was in her own body, but now she was in Achilles's body, too.

Stunned and turned on, she felt the soft silk of her own skin when he touched her breast. She felt her own arousal and also knew the power of his erection as he slid in and out of her.

Before, the friction of him inside her had been enough, but now she experienced the wet heat of her own body as it encased him, the silken feel of her gripping him and the rush of pure pleasure it gave him. She could feel the flow of energy growing as he fed from her.

A shuddering rush rippled through her, spiraling her higher and higher until she reached a point where everything stopped. Then the free fall started. A mind-blowing rush. She cried out.

And before she hit earth, the same spiraling heat lifted her up again twice more.

No way this was just sex. Or lust gone wild. This was something purer, more potent and far more precious.

Achilles could call it an imprint, but she knew what it really was—love.

And as much as she wanted to never leave this feeling, it scared her all the same. Love caused people to make stupid choices. Love got people hurt. But she didn't care.

All she needed, all she desired at the moment, was to feel him and know they were together. That she mattered to him. Tomorrow and the next day could wait.

He pulled away from her, his fangs slipping from her skin. The power still radiated around them, a literal glow in the room. He leaned in, touching his forehead to hers.

"I'm sorry, sweetling. I couldn't stop myself."

"Sorry? Don't be sorry. That was…that was incredible."

A heartbreaking half smile lifted his sculpted lips that had been so soft, so tender against her. "I'm afraid I haven't been the best mentor for you. I wasn't strong enough to hold off the imprint forming between us."

"How could you? Didn't you tell me an imprint was stronger than any one vampire?"

He looked away, unable to meet her eyes and Beck's chest constricted. "I should have let another mentor you." The regret and self-loathing in his voice made her ache for him.

"Look, who says it isn't in our very nature to be meant for this? Weren't you the one who said you can't fault something for its nature?"

He brushed a large hand over his dark blond cropped

hair and cupped the back of his head. "That's different. I had a responsibility to you. You should have had a choice in the matter."

"But I still do." She caressed his jaw and it flexed beneath her fingers as if she'd caused him pain. "I'm going to get that sample of Vanquish, and I'm going to go back to being mortal. If the imprint lasts through that, then maybe you'll consider that it was meant to be. Deal?"

He closed his eyes and sighed. "It would be for the best."

"Achilles." He looked up and gazed at her, the green of his eyes as deep and dark as the cool bottom of a lake. "I don't regret imprinting with you. Not for a moment."

"That's only because you do not know the darker side of it."

Sometimes there was no winning with a man. She dropped her hand and he pulled back from her, leaving her skin exposed to the cool air. But by the look in his eyes, he'd pulled away from more than just her touch. She phased the bathrobe back around her, but it didn't provide the comfort she needed.

Clearly feeling as vulnerable naked as she did, Achilles phased his jeans, shirt and shoes back into place. "I need to see Dmitri and tell him what you're planning to do."

Beck nibbled at her lip and nodded.

"I'll do everything I can to protect you," he said, almost like another apology, then vanished in a curl of dark smoke.

Beck's sigh echoed heavily in the room. "But who is going to protect me from you?"

She wished she had the luxury of curling up in bed or soaking in a hot tub to wash away the hurt building inside her. But there wasn't time. She needed to get a sample of Vanquish tonight.

She closed her eyes, phasing for herself a pair of snug black jeans, a black turtleneck sweater covered with a fitted black leather jacket and flexible black shoes. Normally black wasn't her thing, but regardless of the fact that she intended to be invisible, a little extra camouflage in the dark couldn't hurt.

Concentrating on the grounds just inside the security gates of Genet-X Laboratories, Beck concentrated on the sucking pull. Suddenly the chill of the night air knifed through her lungs. She glanced up at the sheer pale face of the building. A row of lighted windows glimmered on the sixth floor. Beck knew what she had to do. She blew out a harsh breath, bounced on the balls of her feet a time or two before crouching down, then pushed up with all her might. She landed on the window ledge outside the sixth floor laboratory and gazed in at what had once been her desk.

A pang of familiarity hit her in the gut. Her desk looked just the same as she'd left it two weeks ago. Margo looked the same as she had two weeks ago. But two weeks had changed Beck's outlook on the world forever.

Their desks faced each other, but Margo sat at the pair of desks alone, her dark bob hair cut pinned neatly behind her ears. It was late, nearly 10:00 p.m. according to the clock on the laboratory wall. But Beck knew the kind of hours she had to be putting in to get results, especially working on it alone. She lifted her head as the phone rang.

Outside Beck felt the vibration of the phone along the tiny hairs on her arm. She closed her eyes testing her new senses just as Achilles had taught her. At first the rumble of the central heating and air conditioning system mimicked the roar of a jet engine.

Beck tried harder, sorting through sounds. It was like tuning a radio dial to pick up exactly what she wanted to hear.

Finally she caught Margo's staccato voice. "—excellent, bring him to the lab. They should be here shortly. Call me when they arrive." She hung up, then twisted each of the vials in the test tube rack on her desk so that none of the labels matched the same direction.

When *who* arrived? The investors? She'd see for herself soon enough. Beck telescoped her vision so she could easily read the paperwork on Margo's desk. The final approval documents for payment on the project was waiting for signature pending one last satisfactory product test.

Beck closed her eyes, changing focus, then opened them once more as Margo got up from her desk and punched in the security code on the panel. Each button clicked loudly, like someone rapping a door knocker.

Two unfamiliar men, dangerous looking and built

like brick walls, dragged a third man between them, his head covered by a dark hood, apparently unconscious.

"Unbelievable. Now they've resorted to kidnapping," Beck muttered under her breath. The coppery scent of fear joined with peppered anger in the air around her. She'd bet ten to one that whoever was under that sack was a male vampire. How in the hell could they do this? Vampires weren't a subspecies, they were human—a different kind of human, but human.

The cold, salt and kelp-scented air coming off the Puget Sound tugged at her, shifting her feet on the narrow window ledge. She dug her fingers tighter into the concrete, creating little puffs of dust that blew away in the breeze.

The security door sealed shut with a sucking sound. Meathead One and Two plunked the limp vampire into a chair, then roughly pulled his hands behind him securing them with a pair of handcuffs. Fat lot of good it would do them when the vampire woke up mighty pissed. Unless—and the thought disturbed Beck even more—unless they were silver cuffs. Based on how out of it the vampire looked, he'd been given one heck of a dose of corpse cooler.

Achilles hadn't mentioned anything else that could knock out a vampire like this.

"He's secure," said Meathead One. Margo, who'd already returned to her desk, snatched up one of the vials of swirling black and green liquid and slipped it into the pocket of her white lab coat.

Beck ran a quick scenario in her head. She needed to

get closer, grab one of those vials and test it to determine exactly what Margo was planning. If she knocked Margo out after the guards left, she might have enough time to grab one of the vials and get it back to the labs at the clan headquarters.

The phone rang again and Margo pressed the speaker button. "Doctor, your guests are on their way up."

"Thank you."

Crap. Scratch that plan, Beck thought.

Margo glanced at her hired thugs. "You two can wait outside. I may need help with the cleanup."

Pressure throbbed behind Beck's front gums, her fangs pressing for release. It angered her that Margo was being so laissez-faire about the life of another being as if murder were no big deal. What had happened to her? Not just four months ago she and Margo had a conversation about what a better place the world would be when they eradicated the vampire virus. They'd been so secure in their own omniscience that they'd passed over one of the most important tenants of their profession: never assume anything.

Beck pushed the uncomfortable memory away and focused her entire energy on feeling light and as insubstantial as air so she could pass through the wall.

She found herself inside the laboratory. The security door swished open and in came the three investors. Even though she was invisible, Beck backed into the corner out of habit.

"You're going to be very pleased by the results, gentlemen. The new ichor base has presented significant improvements in the formulation for Vanquish," Margo said with pride in her voice.

"I'll believe it when I see it, Dr. Rutledge," Pastor Snyder responded with distain.

Margo unstopped the vial and poured it into a simple spray bottle. The scent of black licorice blended with sour green apples permeated the air. Beck hadn't ever noticed a scent to Vanquish before.

"Please observe that we no longer require it to be injected to be affective," said Margo. "The new formulation for Vanquish is so far improved that it can be administered via a simple spray bottle." She stretched forward and stripped the black hood from the captive sitting in the chair.

"You see, gentlemen, every organism has weaknesses. For vampires, dead man's blood acts as a fast-acting poison. It effectively immobilizes them for several hours once it enters the skin. Silver burns and disrupts muscle and nerve function."

How had Margo learned that, and from whom? The limp head covered in spiky platinum blond hair slowly raised. A pair of dark red eyes bored into Margo, full of hate, vengeance and superiority.

Beck gasped. Vane.

Margo's head tilted a fraction as if she'd heard Beck.

Beck plastered herself against the wall and struggled not to make another sound. Surely Margo hadn't heard her.

"Vampires aren't so very hard to catch, once you

understand the creatures," Margo continued as she shook the nondescript white pump spray bottle in her hand.

Vane spat, fangs coming out in full force, lethal white and dripping venom. The almond scent filled the room, almost cloying to Beck's amped sense of smell. Whatever Margo had given Vane had weakened him, but was wearing off quickly. Margo didn't seem to care. She glanced at the trio of investors. "Once Vanquish is administered, it takes only forty-eight hours or less to complete the transition."

Vane waited until she was within arm's reach then leaped from his chair grabbing her. Margo shrieked, and sprayed him full in the face.

Vane stumbled back, moaning in agony as the skin on his face began to bubble and crisp, as though he were under a broiler. Pungent smoke rose in spirals as his skin blackened. With inhuman cries he fell to his knees, his hands clawing at his head, digging out chunks of charcoal that had once been pale skin and muscle. His features were already charred and undistinguishable. Only his fangs gleamed, brilliantly white, against the blackened husks that were once his lips. The acrid stench and the haze of smoke tainted the air.

Margo backed up against the desk, a hand shielding her mouth and nose from the smoke. In minutes, only his black leather duster and a pile of white-gray ash remained. The central ventilation system had sucked up the smoke with quiet, detached efficiency.

A gag reflex kicked in hard and Beck struggled to hold it in check. She swallowed hard. She hadn't liked Vane.

Truth be known, she hadn't even really known Vane. But in her mind's eye for an instant she had replaced Vane's face with Achilles's and the image had left her terrified. Then she thought of her mother. If Vane had been Victor, she'd just lost the one person who could tell her where her mother was. She had to do something to stop this.

Cardinal Worcher applauded. His eyes glittered with appreciation, his heavy ring winking in the brilliant overhead lighting. "Excellent. Stupendous. A vast improvement. When can we begin shipping it?"

Margo blinked as she stroked her throat, then she brushed back her perfect hair with shaking fingers. Far from being frightened, Margo seemed excited by what had just happened. Eager. "We could begin manufacturing as soon as tomorrow and shipments could begin by the end of the week."

The stout Reverend Evans slapped the painfully thin Pastor Snyder on the back. "Dust to dust." He looked pleased, his fleshy face wreathed in a sadistic, self-satisfied smile. "I timed it. One minute, eighteen seconds. With this antidote we can eliminate the entire vampire population within a month!"

At this moment, Beck would have gleefully watched the whole lot of them fry. What angered her worse than being lied to about the real reason they wanted the vaccine was that they'd used her mind, her abilities, to do something she never would have condoned.

While they congratulated each other, Meathead One and Two were brought back in to sweep up what was left of Vane. Beck picked her way carefully and silently to Margo's desk and snagged a vile of the new and improved Vanquish.

As soon as she palmed the vial, it disappeared. She stuffed it into the interior pocket of her jacket just as a further precaution, then backed slowly toward the wall where she'd entered. Just because she was invisible didn't mean they wouldn't feel her if someone walked into her.

"I believe we've delivered on our agreement," Margo said as she walked toward her desk, just a few feet from where Beck stood. The sour green apple scent of Vanquish clung to her, and it made Beck slightly nauseous. She'd never been so disappointed in her own judgment in her life. She'd trusted Margo. Thought they were on the same team fighting to heal, to help. It proved once more her ability to judge people sucked. She couldn't trust her gut, only what her head told her.

"If you gentlemen could sign for final payment on the project, we'll get Vanquish into production for you as soon as possible."

Clearly Margo had been in it just for the money.

Margo turned, grabbing the paperwork on the desk. Her eyes narrowed as she stared at the rack holding the vials of Vanquish. Her gaze darted quickly around her desk and to the floor. Beck's whole body tightened. Margo knew a vial was missing. "I don't know how you did it, Rebecca," she whispered, barely moving her lips, "but you can't stop it. Nobody can," Margo said under her breath.

Margo's head swiveled around looking straight at

Beck. Then Margo's eyes flashed from dark brown to a pale blue that stunned Beck. Good grief, was Margo possessed?

Beck didn't wait to find out. She focused on phasing through the wall and transporting back to the clan complex on the double.

Have you got the lab on alert? she asked Achilles with her mind.

Ready and waiting for you, Doc.

Good, because there's something weird about all of this.

Concern shimmered through the air and she could feel the tension building in him even though they weren't in the same room.

His voice came through loud and clear, a soldier focused and in control. *I'll be there in five.*

Chapter 15

Achilles scrubbed his hands over his face. "What do you mean her eyes flashed blue?"

"It isn't like I waited to ask Margo questions," Rebecca shot back. She spun around, nearly toppling over a white armchair in her haste and he grabbed her arm to steady her. The atrium's waterfall, meant to be serene, was getting on his nerves.

"Tell me again."

"Her eyes have always been brown. But when she looked at me, it was like a wall of icy water hit me, and her eyes flashed blue. It's illogical. Do you think she could be possessed?" Rebecca asked wryly, her own hazel eyes glinting at the preposterous notion.

But it was not preposterous at all. In fact, Achilles damn well bet on possession. Eris wasn't taking any chances with this pet project of hers. She was going to ensure mass destruction on a global level no matter what it took to feed her hunger. His gut took a dive and hardened into stone. Eris was going to start World War III using vampires against humans. He blew out a harsh breath to steady his nerves and released his hold on Rebecca.

"Got a sample of the ichor?"

She shot him a cool look, but he saw the flash of real fear in her eyes, and in the slight tightening of her soft mouth. "Yes. Of course."

He held out his hand. "Let's have it then."

She stepped back, then took several more steps, separating them by a good ten feet. "No way. Considering what it did to Vane, I want to handle it in a secure, sealed room. No vampires older than a few years allowed. And that includes *you*."

The determination etched into her delicate heart-shaped face was admirable. Her glossy dark curls bounced as she straightened her shoulders. Gods, but she was beautiful when she was focused. Still, no matter how cute she was, there was no way he was letting her take care of this alone.

He walked toward her. Rebecca retreated until her back hit the wall. She scowled a warning. "Stay where you are, Achilles. This stuff is lethal. I don't want you to get hurt."

"I feel the same way about you, sweetling." He teleported the few feet between them, and brushed his fingers across her soft cheek. "It's in a sealed vial, right?"

Rebecca pulled the vial from her jacket pocket and shook it lightly. Malevolent green and black swirled inside the innocuous glass vial. "Do not touch this!"

"For gods' sake, Rebecca. It's sealed."

She growled at him and he stopped. "I'm serious, Achilles. This will destroy you, just like it did Vane."

A cold sense of impending disaster dredged up inside him. "Tell me."

"They captured him and used him as a guinea pig." Her grip tightened on the vial, all but hiding it from view. "This reduced him to ash."

Achilles shifted his weight looking with new respect at the little vial in her hand. "How fast?"

"Less than two minutes."

He took a step backward as if she held a live grenade in her hand. He'd seen the destructive forces of time ravage other vampires during the plague. It was a brutal way to die. He cursed under his breath. "You're right to be cautious. I don't want you near it, either. Put it down. That stuff is lethal."

"Only to vampires like you. I'd just age by a few weeks."

"I have to tell Dmitri."

A curl of dark smoke eddied in the air beside Achilles. "Tell me what?" Dmitri demanded. He twisted his head, his eyes darting from Achilles to Rebecca and back again. He sniffed the air. "Oh, gods. You two have imprinted. You reek of roses and honey."

Achilles put his hand on Dmitri's chest. "The council isn't going to care about that once they see the destruction in a bottle." He glanced at Rebecca. "Tell him what it did to Vane."

As soon as she was finished with her story for the second time, Dmitri's legs wobbled. Achilles managed to phase him a chair in time so he didn't go sprawling on the floor.

He gripped the arms of the chair so hard his knuckles turned white and his fingertips deeply indented the wood. "We don't have a choice. We've got to destroy the lab now, before they begin production and distribution of this weapon. I must tell the council immediately." He shot out of his chair and leveled his gaze at Achilles. "Have a team ready to move."

Achilles gave one curt nod. Dmitri disappeared in a swirl of dark smoke. While neither of them were looking, Beck phased the vial back home and put it in the photo box at the back of her closet where no one would think to look for it.

Achilles closed his eyes and a blast of power radiated out of him that shimmered through her. "The team's been put on alert. I'll have to go."

The twisting deep in Beck's gut increased. "This is far worse than I even imagined, isn't it?"

"You don't know the half of it." Achilles shoved his fingers over his scalp, worry creasing his forehead. "I think Eris has taken over Margo. And if she has, then destroying the lab and everything in it is only going to be a stopgap measure. She's out for total destruction."

Beck sucked in a breath and her body shuddered. "So she won't stop at vampires."

"Hell, no. The more the merrier, as far as she's concerned. She'll pit vampires against humans and feed off both sides. If Eris has her way, she'll use Vanquish to start World War III."

Beck didn't know Eris, but a man like Achilles wasn't scared of much and he seemed terrified of her. She leveled her gaze at him. "What if they've already started manufacturing Vanquish?"

His eyes widened. "Is that possible?"

Beck nodded. "Once Margo got approval, she could overnight samples to a dozen locations nationwide that have the facilities capable of reproducing Vanquish in large batches. It's no different than the manufacturing process of a flu vaccine. Just faster."

Achilles uttered a string of swear words. "Then the council better damn well move quickly with a decision. We'll need to take out as much of the original samples as possible before they are distributed."

"Achilles?"

"Yeah?"

"What if Eris has possessed Margo? Does that mean Margo's going to die?"

His gaze cooled. "If Eris has taken over her body, she's already dead."

Beck flinched. She'd suspected it might be the case when Achilles had first mentioned Eris's ability to possess people. But then another thought hit her like a fist to the stomach. "So my exposure to Vanquish could have been part of her plan all along."

Achilles mouth flattened into a grim line. "Yeah."

Beck sighed. "That makes so much more sense to me. I just couldn't ever understand why Margo would have been so careless about any kind of life, or why she'd gone along with the investors."

"Or why she stabbed you in the back?" He reached out, placing his arm around her shoulders. His hand, warm and comforting, rubbed against her upper arm, soothing her stinging pride. It hurt to know that she'd been betrayed by someone she'd considered a colleague and a friend. Knowing that it had been Eris in a Margo bodysuit made it marginally more tolerable.

"Yeah. That, too." She hesitated as a thought sunk like a stone to the pit of her stomach. Did Eris's plan also include getting Achilles to mentor as a means to destroy him? He certainly was more vulnerable now that he'd imprinted with her. The thought of being used as a tool caused a blend of acrid smoke and pepper to swirl in the air.

Before she could ask how her exposure might interact with the imprint, a curl of dark smoke eddied before them and Dmitri reappeared. Achilles quickly withdrew his arm from around her shoulders. Beck had a sudden flashback to being a teenager and having her mom show up just as her boyfriend was about to kiss her.

Dmitri clapped a hand on Achilles's broad shoulder. "Go time."

"Already?" Beck grabbed hold of Achilles's arm, both hands wrapping around his massive bicep without even overlapping. "Can I come? You'll need to know where to store the samples and the code to get into the temperature-controlled storage vault."

"We'll just phase through the vault wall."

"You don't know what you'd pass on the way through those walls. It could be just as lethal as Vanquish."

"Good point." Achilles cast a questioning glance at Dmitri.

"Can she flux?" The skeptical sound in Dmitri's tone irritated Beck. Even though she wasn't exactly sure what he was asking.

"Flux?" Beck muttered.

Achilles looked at her for a moment. "Go invisible." He turned back to Dmitri. "It's how she got the sample of the vaccine in the first place," he said, a note of pride in his voice.

Dmitri lifted a brow, looking at her with new respect. "Seems the imprint agrees with you, fledgling."

"Perhaps it's not the horrible thing everybody seems to think it is."

Dmitri glowered at her, then turned his huge shoulder to her, effectively blocking her out of his conversation with Achilles, but Beck could hear it loud and clear all the same as Dmitri's voice buzzed inside her head.

Are you sure she won't pose a problem for you?
I can handle it.

"Hello. Standing right here. And I can hear what you're saying." They both turned and stared at her.

Dmitri's gaze grew darker, nearly soulless, and Beck fought off the urge to take a step backward. "I'm concerned that, as a newly imprinted fledgling, you will pose risks to your mentor. If you are harmed, he'll suffer as well. I want to be sure I'm not taking unnecessary risks with my captain and best friend's existence. That okay with you?"

Beck shrunk a little inside herself. Dmitri could be intimidating. She hadn't considered how the imprint might impact Achilles's ability to do his job.

Achilles stepped in between them. "Moot point. I'm not leaving her."

Beck peeped out from behind Achilles's massive shoulder. "Besides, who knows, maybe our powers are going to be even greater together."

Dmitri pinned her with his gaze. "That may be, fledgling, but with greater power comes greater responsibility. I know Achilles's weakness, but I do not know yours."

"Her greatest weakness is being a know-it-all. She's too reliant on that big brain of hers."

Dmitri's mouth tipped up at the outside edge, and a little bit of humor danced behind his eyes. "That's yet one more thing she has in common with Kristin, then."

Beck's chest constricted at the thought of her best friend who was married to Dmitri. If they weren't successful in destroying Vanquish, Kris wouldn't die of the aging process, but her husband would. She knew Kris well enough to know her friend would never be the same again.

"Look, my big brain got us into this mess. It's my

responsibility to help get us out of it. Especially if Margo's been possessed by this Eris chick."

Dmitri's eyes rounded. "Eris?" His gaze flicked to Achilles.

Achilles nodded. "Paints the project in a whole new shade of terrifying, doesn't it?"

Dmitri rolled his shoulders. "You should have told me before I went to the council."

"I didn't have time before you went to the council."

"It matters little at this point. Your directive is still the same. Take out the entire complex. Save what mortals you can. And eliminate the researcher."

"We've got one more wrinkle," Achilles said.

Dmitri's brows drew together. "What?"

Achilles turned to Beck and jerked his head in Dmitri's direction. "Tell him about the production process."

Beck swallowed hard. Before, when she'd told Achilles, it had just been another fact, another bit of information. Now she could see how potentially disastrous it could be. "If Margo's already shipped samples to production facilities, the virus could be ready for distribution nationwide within a week, two tops. There's no way we could find it all."

Dmitri visibly shook and he clapped a hand on Achilles's shoulder. "Go, brother, and be damned careful. Be sure the explosion is contained. Even so, I want you all well away from it before it blows just in case the virus is released."

Achilles turned and held out his hand. "Would you

be willing to brief my team on what we might encounter?"

Beck grasped his hand, wishing he saw things as more than just an imprint between them that would vanish once she was mortal again. "Of course. Let's go." He gave her fingers an affectionate little squeeze and then they were transported.

Beck blinked. She'd never been in this section of the clan complex before. The hallway seemed far older than the rest of it. "Where are we?"

"Out near the Space Needle," he explained, keeping hold of her hand, as he walked north down a long corridor. Water trickled in dark slimy paths down the concrete pillars. It looked nothing like the clean modern portions of the clan complex she'd been in earlier.

"Just how far does the complex go?" she asked, glancing around with interest. The dark hallway was punctuated by shafts of light coming from above. Skylights created from cracked small squares of glass in greens and blues allowed the light, but they were obscured in places by patches of concrete where the missing glass had been filled in. Beck stepped around a pile of rusting piping.

Achilles shrugged. "Twenty-five city blocks, more or less. It was built when a fire took out most of the city in the late 1800s. When they rebuilt the city a whole story above the old city streets, we helped out and made the complex our own. This is what's left of Seattle downtown circa 1889."

The hallway ended in a pale olive green metal door

that looked like it had been salvaged from an old army barracks. The small room, no more than twenty-feet square housed a long wooden table and a wall of high-tech computers, hardware and weapons Beck had never seen previously.

A curl of dark smoke, followed quickly by three more preceded the appearance of four vampires that Beck had not met before all decked out in what looked like black military fatigues.

The tallest one, with black hair cut short and sparkling blue eyes, stood with his legs braced wide apart, and locked his gaze on Achilles. "Reporting in, Captain."

Achilles placed a hand on his shoulder. "This is my security team. James, tactical." The blue-eyed vampire smiled at her.

Achilles moved to the next one in line who had broad shoulders and dangerous tigerlike topaz eyes. "Slade, explosives," Achilles said. Slade nodded once.

Beside him stood a guy who looked like a Russian tank. His dark blond hair was buzzed military short and his eyes were such a pale green they reminded Beck of frozen ice. "This is Mikhail, firearms." Mikhail just stared at her, unnerving Beck.

"And lastly, Titus. Communications." Titus, who was slighter than the other three, but no less muscular, winked, his dark brown eyes brilliant.

"Team, this is our intelligence lead on this mission, Dr. Rebecca Chamberlin."

All five male gazes swiveled in her direction. A whiff of something musky tinged with cedar filtered into the air. Beck's best guess was that the scent was testosterone, but with vampires, who knew?

"The mission tonight is search and destroy. Objective—the labs on the sixth floor of Genet-X Laboratories." A small black laptop phased onto the table, the screen showing photos of the campus. "We need to evacuate the building. Titus, hit the fire alarm system and give us a five-minute countdown. That should clear out as many personnel as possible. Whoever is left will be collateral damage." He shot a glance at Beck when she sucked in a gasp of air. "Live with it."

He turned to Slade. "I want charges set to take out the storage area, and all labs on the sixth floor connected to producing the vaccine.

"Rebecca, where are the best entrance points and where is the vaccine stored?"

Beck leaned in to get a better view of the monitor. She pointed at the stairwell that accessed the area closest to the storage vaults. "This way has locked doors, but would take us there the fastest."

"Locks, no problem," offered up James. He smiled at her. "Any laser grids or security pads?"

"Security pad on the vault access, with fingerprint scan. If they haven't changed the code, I can still access it. The only trick will be getting the fingerprint. I'm sure my access has been pulled."

"Did Margo touch the vial with her bare hands?" Achilles asked.

Beck turned looking over her shoulder at him. "Yeah, actually, she did."

"Perfect. James, pull a set of prints off it and make the skins ASAP."

Beck phased the vial into her palm and reluctantly handed it over to James. "Be careful with it."

James evaporated in a puff of dark particles.

"Mik, we've got a possession to deal with. Not wholly vampire. I want DMDs and silver bullets in all weapons."

"What are DMDs?" Beck blurted.

"Dead Man's Darts. Tranqs filled with dead man's blood." Mikhail's voice was far deeper and more graveled than Beck had expected. His green stare was deep and penetrating, making Beck shiver.

Slade bumped Mikhail aside with his shoulder and took a look at the screen. "C-4 or nitroglycerin shots?"

Achilles tapped a key bringing up a schematic of the building's floor plan. "We only want to take out the sixth floor. Not the whole building."

Slade nodded.

A cloud of dark smoke knitted into the broad shoulders and blue eyes of James. "Here's those skins, Chief." He handed soft translucent bits of fingertip-sized flexible plastic to Achilles and the vial to Beck. Beck phased the vial back to its hiding place before anyone could ask questions.

"Perfect."

"Rebecca, once we're inside we'll need you to tell us the access codes."

"Wait. What do you mean tell you? I'm going in with you."

Again five pairs of very male, very vampire eyes stared at her as if she were a lone plasmid circulating in a petri dish. "What?"

Slade turned his gaze to Achilles. "She isn't coming in, is she?"

He said "No" just as Beck answered "Yes."

"Look, the timing on this has to be perfect or the security grid will kick in. If you want to get into that vault, you're going to need to know exactly what you're looking for. And maybe it's a guess, but unless any of you here have been a vampire less than five years, anybody bumps or cracks one of those vials before we get out and they're going to turn into dust sooner than later."

"How lethal is this stuff?" Titus asked Beck, his mouth a serious line.

"Very. It took Vane out in less than two minutes."

Slade whistled long and low and Mikhail glowered, his thick brows knitting to a deep V as he clicked the clasps on his pack. James drummed his fingers on the table. "Are we going in with haz suits on?"

Achilles nodded. "Given what the doc has seen, I think it'd be best."

James grunted, then phased in six black hazard suits completed with face panes. He handed them out, but when it came to Rebecca she held up her hands. "Thanks. Don't need one." James's gazed flicked to Achilles.

Achilles shrugged. "Doc knows what she's doing, let her go with it." The suit evaporated into the thin air.

"Suit up and transport on my count in five. Everyone link up. Follow Doc's lead." Achilles touched his watch, setting a countdown, yanked on his suit then held out his hand to her. Beck grabbed his hand and held it hard. One by one his team grasped the person's shoulder in front of them, making it look like some bad boy conga line ready to kick ass.

"Ready to fly, Doc?"

Beck nibbled on her lip. "Not like we have a choice, is it?"

Once she was transported, she landed with a thud when they hit the wet grass, the moon a thick crescent overhead in the dark sky. They crouched low to the ground.

"From here on out, mind link only." Everyone in the team nodded.

Do you think she can even flux yet? Beck heard James's voice loud and clear in her head.

Captain wouldn't have her with us if she couldn't, Slade answered back.

She sure wasn't worried about fluxing. Beck wondered how in the world she could sneak into Genet-X with five enormous male vampires and not have security bat an eyelash.

But by now she should've known vampires weren't like anyone else. They moved more like shadows than men. One minute they were at the edge of the fencing, the next they were up against the wall. Beck pushed herself to move quickly, just as Achilles had taught her. The exertion was exhilarating.

The men jumped in turn up the vertical wall to the sixth story in one enormous leap, hanging out on the ledge like a murder of crows waiting for her to join them. Beck crouched, bunching the muscles of her legs and looked up, putting all her focus on making it to the group waiting for her. She released the spring coiled tight inside her and shot upward, the night air stinging and cold as she flew to the sixth floor. Ichor pumped hard and fast through her.

Clinging to the concrete with her fingertips, she glanced over her shoulder down at the six-story drop. Her legs wobbled.

Whoa there, Doc. Put your eyes on me, Achilles said in her head as he grasped her upper arm, pulling her closer to the warmth of his body. Everything grew steady and stronger within her, a fresh flood of power pumping through her at his touch.

Beck grinned. *That was cool!*

He returned her smile and touched her curls. *Hang on, we're going to flux and phase into the building.*

She nodded. Even knowing the plan, it still shocked her when five enormous men suddenly evaporated into nothingness.

You sure you're ready for this? Achilles's voice tickled her ear.

You bet. She focused on becoming lighter than air and found she could no longer see her hands holding on to the concrete wall in front of her. She pushed through the wall, letting the thick gelatinous feel of it slide around her as she moved. The lab looked exactly the same as it had when she'd left it, except for the large black scorch mark that marred the floor where Vane had disintegrated.

She glanced around, but saw no one. A bubble of panic welled up in her chest.

An invisible large warm hand curled around her upper arm in a firm grip. While she couldn't see it, she could definitely feel it, and from the sparks traveling through her she knew it was Achilles. *We're all here with you. Where are the storage vaults?*

Storage vaults are through that door to the right, she answered.

Good. James, pull the fire alarm then follow Doc to the vaults. Titus, start the countdown and tap into their security center. Block the security cameras and any sensors they've got out in the halls on this level. I want us in and out of here in ten minutes. Slade, start setting the explosives. The vault, this lab and the next one over get the hardest hit.

The beeping of a code being punched into the security pad sounded. *Up against the walls. Someone's coming in!* Beck screamed in her head, knowing they all heard her.

The door opened with a swish of air. Margo entered, dressed in street clothes, rather than a lab coat. *Get what you need, then go away,* Beck muttered in her mind. The door suctioned shut. Oh, no. The realization that everyone could hear what she thought came a nanosecond too late.

Margo turned, her gaze vividly blue and trained directly where Beck stood. "Leave? Why would I do that when I came here for you, Rebecca?"

Chapter 16

Six vampires reappeared instantly, filling the room. Achilles stepped between Beck and Eris masquerading as Margo. "You'll go through us to get her." The edge of Achilles's voice was sharper than a blade.

Margo's skin started to sag, looking eerily like it was melting, then peeled off in long strips. A blonde Eris wriggled out of what was left of Margo, leaving the discarded human body boneless and pooled on the floor.

Bile, hot and acidic, surged up Beck's throat. She swallowed hard.

Eris's clear blue eyes rested intently on Beck, sparkling with pleasure. "While that's tempting, Achilles, I have another use for all of you that'll leave me far more satisfied. What I want right now is Rebecca. Without her you don't have a chance of fighting off Vanquish."

"Open fire!" Achilles yelled, and simultaneously cupped his hand over the back of Beck's head and shoved her to the floor, putting himself between her and the goddess. The air above her whizzed and chattered with flying silver bullets and darts as Slade, Mikhail and Titus opened fire from behind them.

Eris shivered but, undaunted, she continued walking slowly and steadily toward Beck and Achilles, her eyes twin points of electric blue flame.

A series of fire alarms wailed to life. Out in the hallways the quick shuffle of footsteps and screams could be heard as people hurried from the building, their fear thick in the air.

"Did you do that just for me?" Eris asked with false sweetness. "I do so *love* panic."

"Hardly." Achilles held up a hand signaling the men to stop their fire.

The bullets and DMDs had torn her thigh-high black patent leather boots and a red skintight satin jumpsuit but left her untouched. Her voice boomed through the lab, causing test tubes to rattle and the windows to vibrate. "Stand aside, Achilles."

"Screw you." Achilles reached into his back pocket.

Eris held out a hand and the lab tables began to shudder and shake, then lifted and slammed against the walls, clearing her path. "Give. Her. To. Me."

Achilles's eyes narrowed into green daggers. "Not a chance."

Her eyes glittered. "Fabulous. I haven't felt you this angry in ages. I've missed your rage, Achilles. It's delicious."

"Don't push your luck, Eris." Achilles fingered a length of chain, small links of a brass-colored metal interlaced with silver ones, and palmed it in his gloved hand. "If you touch her, I'll string you up and return you to Gormorlath."

Eris's eyes narrowed, her beautiful features growing hard. "Don't insult me, vampire. No one will imprison me again." She lifted her chin in disdain.

He let a loop of the metallic chain slide from his fist, the hiss of links sliding against one another sounded ominous. "Wanna bet? I've got a chain with your name on it."

Her blue eyes strayed to the chain, moving slightly as they followed the swing of it. Her blond hair rose, the ends of it writhing about like snakes, but she took a step back. "Keep the bitch. But be warned, Achilles, when I release my new plague among the vampires, you'll be among the first to die and she'll be left a halfling to do my bidding."

She turned on the spot, vanishing into a dark cloud that dissipated into nothingness.

Achilles glanced back at his men. "Seven minutes, people. Mik, stay here and make sure that Eris is truly gone. The rest of you, move out."

He yanked Beck up from the floor and hurried her to the door leading to the vaults. "Work fast, Doc," he ordered as he broke into a fast jog down the hall, heading the way she indicated. They plowed through a set of smaller labs heading toward the center of the building.

Their path ran into the two-foot-thick doors that secured the vault. Beck tapped in the security code. Achilles stopped her hand, his thumb rubbing quick and light over her palm making her shiver. "Put these on first." He slipped the plastic fingerprint clones James had made over her fingertips, checked them for fit and indicated the pad. "Go."

She pressed her thumb and forefinger to the scanner. She counted off the seconds for the red light to turn green, and the locking mechanism to click. It was the longest five seconds of her life.

The instant it did, she let out a sigh and pushed down on the locking handle to release the door.

"Five minutes. Go," Titus said, even his words coming in a rush.

Beck stepped in Achilles's way as he moved to enter ahead of her. As much as she wanted to return to normal, she didn't want him to be harmed. It would be one thing to be without him and another to know he was gone forever. "I'm the only one going in. If you want it to blow, tell me what to do."

Achilles glanced at Slade. "You got a package she can take in?"

Slade nodded and handed the gray block of puttylike substance to her, two thin wires stuck into it along with some sort of digital mechanism. "Just put the charge underneath the part you want to blow. We'll detonate as soon as we're clear. It'll incinerate the vault and most of this floor."

Beck's fingers trembled. Achilles cupped her hand. "You sure you don't want us to go in with you?"

Beck looked up at him, loving that he was worried for her, even now. But this was something only she could do without risking her existence. "I've got it."

She held the block gingerly in her hands as she entered the vault, her eyes scanning the shelves for labeling that would tell her where they'd stashed the Vanquish serum.

Toward the back she found it, a refrigerator-size cabinet full of small tubes. Beck gasped. There was so much of it. What if when it blew, it went up into the atmosphere and took out all the vampires within the city? She felt her stomach knot. Near the bottom rack, nine empty holes stared back at her where there should have been test tubes.

"Four minutes!" From her position inside the vault, Titus's voice sounded like it came from down a tunnel. Beck placed the block of explosives underneath the large cabinet and shut the door. She hurried out of the vault and sealed the door.

"Is there any way we can contain the explosion?"

"Why?" James asked, stepping up beside Achilles.

"There's enough Vanquish in there to take out every vampire in the Pacific Northwest if it gets blown up into the wind. I just want to make sure what we're about to do isn't worse than taking it and destroying it in another way."

"You mean like a dirty bomb?" Slade asked.

Beck nodded.

Slade muttered a curse.

"The heat of the blast will vaporize it on contact," Achilles said. "We'll be fine as long as we're out of the blast zone."

In the distance, fire engine sirens began to wail.

"Two minutes," Titus chimed in.

"Mik, cover us as we exit. There are going to be a lot of mortals out on the grounds. Do what you can to keep them back from the building. The rest of you flux and transport to headquarters."

Everyone nodded. Achilles grabbed Beck's hand and pulled her along with him, fluxing in midstride so that she was holding hands with the invisible man. Beck focused, as she jogged to keep up with his long stride, and fluxed, as well.

"One minute," Titus announced.

A second later, they were back out on the ledge, invisible to the bystanders crowded below. "Move quick."

All six of them jumped. The fall took Beck by surprise, and a blast of heat and force from behind shoved her to her hands and knees.

The explosion sent an orange fireball and plume of black smoke shooting up fifty feet into the sky. The people around her screamed, rushing and pressing back from the building. But before she could get caught up in the melee, Beck felt herself transport.

She found herself breathless in the same meeting

room they'd been in before. Titus, James, Slade and Achilles were there with her, and Dmitri joined them.

"The council wants a report, Captain." He directed both his gaze and his words at Achilles.

Achilles phased away the hazard suit, and came to attention. The other men followed his lead. "The mission was successful despite Eris's attempt to sabotage it, *Trejan*."

"So it was as you feared. Eris had possessed the scientist."

Achilles shifted his weight from one foot to the other. "Yes."

"And were you able to subdue her?" Dmitri's gaze flicked from one team member to another looking for answers. The tension in the room grew, pressing in on Beck, making her want to squirm.

"Silver bullets and DMDs passed right through her, *Trejan*," Slade answered.

Dmitri's gaze pinned Slade to the spot where he stood. "She withstood an all-out tactical assault?"

Slade nodded once, the harsh overhead lighting casting shadows beneath his eyes and making the deep crease in his chin look more like a dark slash.

"Hell." Dmitri uttered the word beneath his breath. Somehow from the twist in her gut Beck guessed it was both an epithet and a summary of where the danger emanated from.

Beck scooted closer to Achilles. "Eris isn't just some super vampire, is she?"

Slade looked over at Beck. "She's a goddess. Truly

immortal. But we hoped the silver would disrupt her enough to keep her at bay."

"She doesn't react to silver. It's the orichalcum that does it," Achilles said quietly, the rumble of his words reaching into her. Uncertainty and doubt collected around Achilles like a thick blanket. Beck fought off the sensation, knowing she was somehow reacting empathically to Achilles.

"But was the storage of Vanquish destroyed?" Dmitri pushed.

"What there was of it," Beck said grimly. "There were nine vials missing from the storage locker. My guess is that they've already been shipped out for reproduction at other facilities."

Dmitri's brow creased, his thick brows drawing down. For a moment everything was silent. Dmitri cast his dark gaze in her direction. "Can you give me a list of the possible locations?"

"Of course." Without thinking, she phased a notepad and pen, and wrote quickly.

Another dark curl of smoke wedged its way into the crowded room and Mikhail appeared. "We lost only the one mortal, Captain. The one Eris had possessed. Firemen and several news crews appeared just before I left."

Dmitri turned to Achilles. "If there are news crews, then we're out of time. We need to report this to the council. Now."

There was no way she was being left out of this. Beck stood up a little straighter, pushing her way into the conversation. She might be planning on being a vampire for only a little while longer, but she was still one now. "Then you'll need to take me. I'm the only one who went in the vault."

Achilles grasped her hand. "Better prepare yourself. They're going to know we've imprinted the moment we appear."

She looked in his eyes and tightened her grip on his hand. "Somebody needs to remind them we've got bigger things to worry about."

This time Beck was ready and waiting for the sensation of being transported and soon found herself standing before the set of huge black double doors emblazoned with the red interlaced triple circles. Of course those circles meant something totally different to her now, reminding her of the imprint she and Achilles shared.

The two guards on either side opened the doors letting the three of them walk in as a unit. Achilles still hadn't let go of her hand. Beck's heart swelled. The last time they'd been before the council, he'd tried hard to make sure their imprint wasn't obvious. Perhaps he was holding her hand in a gesture of support or of defiance. Either way she found it comforting, especially as they entered the intimidating presence of the council.

As they passed through the double doors, the candles in their ornately scrolled wrought-iron candelabras flickered with the movement of the air. All nine of the carved cherrywood chairs in the semicircle around the raised dais were occupied by the council members.

Roman sat in the largest and most ornate chair, his face dark and brooding.

The cloying sweetness of the beeswax candles didn't cover the coppery tang of fear that lingered inside. But Beck couldn't tell if it was her own fear she smelled or that of the council members. She glanced at the dark vampire on Achilles's right, the heavy weight on her shoulders lightening a little. Dmitri was clearly there to stand beside her and Achilles in support. They stepped up to the dais and faced the nine carved chairs, each occupied by a vampire with a far too intense gaze.

Beck glanced at Dmitri and Achilles. Both had bowed their heads. She ducked her head, embarrassment heating her face. As fierce as she felt about her imprint with Achilles, she realized that she was on unfamiliar ground.

There were still things about being part of a vampire society she didn't understand, and probably never would.

Dmitri stood tall and took one step forward to address the council. "My Laird, and lords of the council, we have wiped out the main storage and development of the vaccine known as Vanquish. The facility has been eliminated per the council's instructions."

"And the vaccine has been destroyed entirely?" prodded Roman, the clan's laird.

"Not exactly, my Laird," Achilles added, as he, too stepped forward. "My fledgling, who was affiliated with the original vaccine's production—" he glanced back at Beck "—ascertained that nine vials were missing from the storage vault at the lab and may have been delivered to different production facilities across the nation. If this is accurate, then we'll have at most a month before it could be made available on a large scale."

"She's hardly your fledgling. Judging by the scent, you have fully imprinted with one another, is this correct?"

"Yes, my Laird, but—"

"But we will await the judgment on that matter. Dr. Chamberlin is correct. We have bigger problems." Roman waved a hand and a large flat screen television appeared.

Beck stared at the female reporter who was standing in front of a burned-out building while the orange light of the fire still burned brightly against the early morning sky.

The image widened, and the reporter turned, talking to the painfully thin man beside her. He was bundled in a thick tan wool jacket and had his gloved hands clasped together in front of him.

Pastor Snyder.

His supercilious manner oozed through the screen, as he looked down at the reporter who was a foot shorter.

"Is it true, Pastor Snyder, that the destruction of the building was caused by a group of protestors out to destroy the research paid for by the Foundation for the Greater Good?"

"Yes, Lynn, but despite the destructive efforts of the vandals, our efforts to protect the American public have still been successful. Fortunately, not all of the vaccine was on the premises at the time of the explosion." He pressed his fingers together so they formed a steeple. "Shortly it will be available to the public."

He gave a good attempt at a smile, but Beck could tell he was only doing it for the camera. Snyder was worried about something. Perhaps cutting a deal with Eris wasn't turning out as clean and neat as they'd anticipated.

"There you have it. Back to you, Jeff."

The television vanished as quickly as it had appeared. Roman narrowed his gaze and asked Beck, "How dangerous is this vaccine in its improved form?"

She swallowed hard against the thickness in her throat. Being the messenger stank, especially when it was to a bunch of powerful vampires who were going to be good and angry about the news. "Any vampire older than a few years could potentially age to their true chronological form in less than forty-eight hours."

The air buzzed with several low conversations between the different members of the council. Roman held up his hand and silence returned to the chamber.

"What are our chances of defending ourselves against this vaccine should we not be able to discover its whereabouts before distribution?"

Beck sucked in a steadying breath and lifted her gaze to meet Roman's. "Unless I can create an antidote before distribution begins, none."

Chapter 17

The dark granite walls of the council chamber seemed to be closing in. All the council members wore looks of horrified disbelief.

"Are you claiming, Dr. Chamberlin, that there is no cure, no antidote for this?" one of the vampires asked.

"Not yet. The vaccine is genetically based on the plague. Something you've all been exposed to for centuries, which means this strain is nearly perfect in its ability to single out the vampire virus and activate the deadly aspects of its genetic encoding."

A low murmur of voices hummed in the room, amplified by the walls and large proportions of the chamber.

"You're claiming the plague has returned?" demanded one of the lords of the council, his long white hair swinging as he leaned forward, snowy brows drawn down over red eyes.

Beck swallowed. "Scientifically speaking, yes."

Roman sat stiffly, his gaze touching briefly with each of the council members before coming back to lock on to her face. "By unanimous decision of the council, we would ask that you immediately begin working on an antidote. Not just for our clan, but to protect all our kind. It's a challenge, but we believe you are the best choice to fight against it."

Beck grasped her hands together in front of her. Achilles's hand, warm and strong, settled on her shoulder.

"My lords, I would ask on behalf of Dr. Chamberlin, that in return for her efforts, you grant her amnesty from any charges related to our imprinting."

Beck stiffened. In her worry over the impact of the vaccine, she'd forgotten the warning the council had issued the last time she'd been in this chamber.

"My lords," she blurted. "I have my own request. I'd ask that you spare my mentor any charges because of our imprinting. It was my choice. Not his."

The buzz, sounding like a swarm of angry bees, started up again, but then suddenly stopped as Roman rose from his ornately carved seat. He stepped forward and bent to one knee in front of Beck, gazing up at her face. "My lady, if you can indeed preserve our kind with your knowledge and effort against this new plague, then I, indeed all of us, would be greatly indebted to you. We would of course grant you and your mentor amnesty."

Beck, not knowing exactly what the etiquette was in such matters, executed a little curtsy. "Thank you, my lords."

His brow furrowed with worry, Roman rose, then grasped her hand between both of his. The air around him had the musty smell of sorrow. "However, you must be aware, Doctor, though we may forgive the civil infraction you have committed, there is nothing that can be done to change the effects of the imprint once it has been made. Whatever he suffers, so shall you. Whatever powers he has, so shall you share in them. And if, and when, death should claim one of you, the other shall be condemned to the existence of a halfling. In these things there is nothing that can be done to protect you."

Beck nodded, leaning into Achilles's side, drawing closer to him for strength. "I knew that going into the imprint and I still did it. It is my hope that if I turn back to mortal that Achilles will be spared those problems."

Roman gave her hand a small squeeze. "Then so be it."

Both Achilles and Dmitri placed their forearms across their chests, hands closed into fists in a form of salute and bowed to the council. Awkwardly, and a few seconds behind, Beck did, too.

A guard rose to the dais to escort them from the chamber and Beck fell into line behind Achilles.

Is she experienced and knowledgeable enough to create an antidote? Dmitri's voice echoed in Beck's head.

Can you think of anyone else who'd even have a shot? Achilles answered.

Take her to the laboratories in the medical center. I'll alert the staff that they are to help her in whatever she requires.

Achilles nodded, then glanced back at her, his lips twitching. "Do I need to repeat any of that, or did you hear it all loud and clear, Doc?"

Her heart did a double *bump thump*. He was so strong, so kind, so responsible—in short the perfect guy—*if* he'd been human, *or* she'd wanted to stay a vampire. Beck cracked a weak smile at him. "Do you want to walk to the medical center or shall we transport?"

"Enjoying your newly developed powers, are you?"

Beck shrugged. "As long as I'm a vampire, I might as well use my skills while I have them, right?"

A hurt look flickered for an instant across Achilles's strong face. "Be careful working with that vaccine. Don't take any chances."

Beck crossed her arms. "What's the worst that happens? I go back to being mortal just a little earlier than we planned?"

Achilles's jaw flexed. She waited for him to say something, anything. She reached out, trying to listen to his thoughts and found herself suddenly and effectively blocked.

"Why are you blocking me?" she asked, her tone a little acerbic.

"So you can focus. The antidote is all that matters right now. Let's get you to work."

Baloney. Beck wasn't stupid before, and she certainly

hadn't become so in the last five minutes. Achilles wasn't telling her everything.

Before she could push the issue with him further, he vaporized into a dark mist. She sighed, then transported herself to the medical center's atrium.

The receptionist didn't look the slightest bit fazed that two vampires just popped into existence in front of her desk. Guess it happened enough it was simply normal.

"This is Dr. Chamberlin. She's to be given black level access to all laboratories and materials."

The receptionist nodded, tucking her sweep of smooth dark hair behind her ear. "*Trejan* Dionotte has already put us on alert. Please, will you follow me?"

She came out from behind her desk and Beck took two steps to follow her before she realized Achilles hadn't moved.

"Aren't you coming with me?"

He shook his head. "I've got other duties to attend to. If you aren't successful, the council will probably call for an all-out war against the mortals holding the vaccine."

Beck stiffened. "It's probably better if you don't come. I wouldn't want you to be exposed." Even if she would have appreciated the support of having him there, the lab was going to be off-limits to all vampires until she knew precisely what she was dealing with in Margo's version of the vaccine.

She reached out to him, to tell him to cross his fingers for her, and found herself still blocked. Her heart twinged. She'd come to rely too heavily on the special bond between them and she suddenly realized how hard it was going to be when it was gone.

He nodded, his mouth forming a grim line. "Good luck, Doc." And just like that, he disappeared.

The receptionist stared back, waiting, and Beck trotted to catch up to her. "Dr. Shepperd is waiting for you in the lab. Ask him for anything you require and he'll see that it's obtained for you immediately, Dr. Chamberlin."

She swung open the metal doors to reveal a tall man with a warm smile and wire-rimmed glasses. His dark hair was military short and he wore a spotless white lab coat.

Beck smiled at the receptionist as she turned to leave. "Thank you."

The vampire held out his hand. "Dr. Alastair Shepperd, at your service." His British accent made Beck smile a little as he executed a little bow from the waist in a way that was centuries out of date.

"I'm guessing you aren't originally from the Seattle area."

He nodded, returning her smile. "But I daresay I've been here far longer than you, if the stories are true." He began to walk down the carpeted hallway toward a set of white double doors at the far end. Translucent walls of backlit frosted glass glowed softly, illuminating the windowless space.

"Just how long?" Beck asked curiously. He looked about forty, but vampires never showed their age. Except for Vane right up until the end. Beck shivered in the climate-controlled space. She had to find the cure.

Had to. *Nothing* must happen to Achilles. She'd work tirelessly, night and day to find a cure.

Sheppard smiled. "Two hundred and thirty-six years, give or take a month or two. I was a surgeon for the redcoats on the Eastern seaboard. I spent some time as an early explorer and eventually made my way to the west coast. I can still tell you this country is nothing like I've ever seen."

"In that case, you might want to make sure you don't come into the lab with me. I've seen this vaccine reduce a far older vampire than you to dust in less than two minutes."

His mouth dropped open a little. "I say," he breathed.

"That's one reason I'll need a sealed lab and strict access restrictions for all personnel."

They pushed through the double doors and the hallway became a stark, sterile, ubiquitously white clean room. Dr. Shepperd keyed a code into the security pad. "I'm clearing the code to this lab for your exclusive use. Please select any sequence you wish. If you'll compose a list of items you'll require, I shall have them delivered to you within the hour."

"Can I phase within the lab?"

His eyes crinkled at the corners. "Of course you may. I wasn't given an indication of your ability levels. Should you require anything, please ring me." He handed her a business card with his name and an extension printed on it. "Simply dial nine on the phone inside the lab and then my extension and it will ring me directly."

Beck took the card and slipped it into her pants

pocket. "Thanks. I'd better get to work." She turned to the keypad and entered the same code as the one she'd had at Genet-X. The door swished open and Beck stepped inside. The lab was twice as nice as anything she'd had at Genet-X and outfitted to the hilt.

She phased the vial of Vanquish she'd taken from Margo's desk into her hand and set to work. "Let's see exactly what Eva's ichor did to you," she murmured as she slipped on a pair of gloves, her goggles and a lab coat, then unstoppered the bottle. She used a pipette to withdraw a small amount of the vaccine and smear it on a glass slide.

Underneath the microscope, the vampiriophages were still present. Beck upped the magnification of the electron microscope and saw a subtle difference. Instead of only six strands of long tails, there were eight, two far shorter than the others, like little fangs.

All afternoon Beck examined and peeled apart the vaccine, looking at the PCR substitution Margo had performed. "You did a good job for a dead woman," she said to no one in particular. Per her request, no one had entered the lab while she'd been there. The seclusion was a both a blessing and a curse as every moment she spent working on the antidote was a minute closer to her becoming mortal again.

The work dragged on for hours. A painful twisting sensation bit into her midsection and Beck realized she hadn't eaten in far too long. The thought of drinking a pint of blood didn't seem appealing in the slightest, so instead she phased herself a pepperoni pizza while she waited for the centrifuge to finish separating the DNA from the sample of vaccine.

Usually it was a huge no-no to eat in a lab. Too many things could easily contaminate both the food and the samples. But since she was alone, Beck refused to worry about it. She sucked down four slices of pizza before she realized that the pinching, twisting sensation was only growing worse rather than going away.

"Bet nothing but blood will do it," she muttered under her breath as she phased away the rest of the pizza and replaced it with a glass filled with a Bloody Mary, heavy on the blood. She shuddered and grasped the glass. "Bottoms up, Doc."

Holding her nose with one hand, she chugged the contents of the glass. "Ugh. Revolting."

The pain speared red hot through her middle and Beck gasped at the sensation, dropping the dirty glass to the floor. It shattered in a spray of shards.

The centrifuge chimed, indicating her samples were ready to review. Beck scraped herself together and slogged over to the machine, groaning against the ache that was now taking over her joints. A throb behind her eyes made her squint in the bright light of the lab.

Why was she hurting so badly? She'd eaten, hadn't she?

That's when the thought struck her so soundly it made her numb from head to toe. Dear God. This wasn't her pain.

Achilles.

Beck didn't think about it. She just put her mind out

and tried to reach him. But the block was still firmly in place. Wherever he was, he didn't *want* her to reach him.

"I don't think so, tough guy." Beck stalked out of the lab double time, all the while yelling for Achilles with her mind.

Dr. Shepperd bolted out of adjoining door in the hallway and nearly ran her over. "Are you all right?"

"I need to see Achilles. Now."

Dr. Shepperd took one look at her and visibly blanched. "Yes. Of course. Right away."

He grasped her shoulder and transported her to a hallway filled with doors.

"This is our intensive care unit. He collapsed about fifteen minutes ago." Shepperd twisted the doorknob and opened the pale wooden door.

Achilles lay in a hospital bed, his face a waxen image of his former self. She stepped to his side.

"Oh, my God." Her hand shook as she brushed it along the edge of his hairline and his square jaw. "What's happening to you?"

He cracked open his eyes and attempted a weak smile. "Dying."

All the strength left her body in a rush leaving her deflated like a used plasma bag. "But you weren't even exposed."

"No. But you were. I told you there was a dark side to imprinting. We share everything now, Rebecca. Power and pain. Life and death. You were exposed while working in the lab, so now I'm reacting to it just as if

I'd been right there with you. You're returning to your mortal state bit by bit."

"No! That's not possible. You would have told me if there was a risk."

His eyes softened, vulnerable and sad.

Beck muttered a few choice curse words under her breath. Fear making her body hot then cold. "How am I supposed to fight something I don't even understand?"

He brushed his fingertips over the curve of her face, his thumb tracing across her cheek in a tender way that made her chest ache with longing. "Use what you know. You're brilliant, Rebecca. If anyone can find the answer, I know it's you."

"But I need more time."

He closed his eyes, held them shut for a second, then gazed deeply into her face. "Time is one thing vampires can't control."

Chapter 18

Inside Achilles was a seething, roiling mass of agitation, regret and frustration. He hated being useless. He'd known that there'd be every chance that the imprint would impose its darkness over him once more, and yet for Rebecca he'd been willing to risk it.

Why? Why did this one female completely flip him end for end? Yes, she was Ione reborn, but it was more than that. Lying in the hospital bed, even with the most excellent of care, didn't help matters. It gave him an annoyingly large amount of time to reflect.

His destiny was to be a halfling. Hers to be mortal. Period. Imprint or not.

The nurse sampled his ichor once more, drawing a syringe of the black liquid from his veins. She didn't bother to cover the spot with a cotton ball or bandage.

Vampires healed so quickly it would have been a useless gesture.

But Achilles knew he wasn't an average vampire anymore. Being a halfling was something different. Being imprinted, something different again. The only chance he and Rebecca both had of staying sane, because neither of them would ever be whole, was for her to return to her mortal state and he to his halfling existence. At least then if he had to live as a halfling, he could serve the clan and his kind.

That was *if* he could. If the imprint worked the way the doctors had been whispering about in the hall, he didn't have much time to worry about it. His body was already aging. That didn't happen to healthy vampires. That hadn't happened the first time, when Ione had died.

Rebecca had already been at work a week on the vaccine sample and tried a half dozen substitutions and manipulations of the virus. She looked as worn out as he felt. Which was likely true. She hadn't said anything each night when she'd come to sit with him for an hour or two, but he could see the pain and suffering etched into the smoothness of her skin, and the dark smudges growing beneath her eyes. The imprint was taking its toll on her, as well. They were both suffering.

The nurse left and flipped on the television as she exited his room. He'd been watching the mortal news to see how close Eris and her group of stooges were to getting Vanquish manufactured and released.

Every day he'd watched. Every day he'd breathed a

sigh of relief that Rebecca had one more day to create the antidote they needed.

But today it looked as if their luck had run out.

"Ms. Diva, you said that your organization has found a cure for the vampirism virus?" the reporter sitting across from Eris prompted.

Gods, she didn't even bother to disguise her identity for any that knew it. She was using Diva—Latin for goddess—as a last name. He could only imagine the panic this would incite among vampires, and the mob mentality it would stir up among mortals. She must be gorging on the chaos.

"That's right, Jane." The camera shifted in for a close-up that revealed a glimmer of utter delight in the depths of Eris's eyes. "Not only has the Foundation for the Greater Good undertaken the financing for research to produce the vaccine, but we've gone a step further. It'll be available starting tomorrow."

Achilles just about fell out of his hospital bed. Tomorrow?

He groaned. His chest constricted, ribs nearly cracking from the viselike sensation. He closed his eyes hoping it would all just go the hell away.

"You're not sounding so good." Rebecca's voice rippled through him, bringing awareness to his ragged senses. The spicy scent of her skin and hair, the sweetness of the lip balm she always wore, the heat of her beside his bed, her hand, so soft, covering his.

Achilles opened his eyes. "Hey, Doc. How goes the battle?"

She nibbled at her lip, making him wish she'd bend down just a bit more so he could kiss her. He could use a kiss about now.

Beck's brow lifted. "Is that so?" She bent down and gave him a sweet lingering kiss.

Damn. He must be slipping. He'd been doing so well at blocking her. His strength was ebbing, gradually, completely and he was doing everything he could from having it impact her.

"Eris was on the evening news hailing the wonders of Vanquish and its availability tomorrow."

Rebecca sucked in a startled breath. "I'm so close, so close. I just need a little more time."

"Sorry, sweetling, like I said—"

"Yeah, yeah, I know. Vampires can't control time." She sighed as she twisted the end of an auburn curl around her fingers.

"All the better reason you should be at the lab rather than wasting your time sitting here."

Anger flared in her eyes. "I'm *not* wasting my time with you."

"Yes, but you being here isn't helping anyone, is it?"

"Why do you keep trying to block me, to shut me out?"

Achilles turned his head away from her looking toward the translucent glass wall. "You know."

"It's because I'm still planning on returning to being mortal, isn't it?"

He turned back, taking in the sweet curve of her cheek, the dark fringe of her lashes around her too bright eyes and realized with a hitch in his gut that she was about to cry.

"Don't cry, sweetling." He reached out to brush away the tear already tracking a wet trail down her cheek.

She swatted his hand away, her face crumpling. "You don't get it, do you? I love you. I don't understand why we can't remain together even if I'm human and you're still a vampire."

Achilles sighed soul deep. He wished to the gods that there were easy answers. "You don't love me, sweetling. That's just the imprint talking. You'll go back to being mortal. You'll be free of me, and hopefully free of this imprint. And you'll have a normal life."

She shook her head, curls bouncing with the move ment. "No," she said simply, then worried the edge of her lip with her teeth. She glanced at the ceiling and sniffed, then harshly wiped the back of her hand across her eyes. "I'll never be free of you. Being mortal isn't the issue here and you know it. You're just afraid."

"Spartan warriors aren't afraid." It was a good try, but his bravado sounded false even to his own ears.

"News flash. You're not a Spartan. You're a vampire in the twenty-first century. You're afraid of love. I get that. Love sometimes opens you up to a lot of hurt."

Achilles grumbled. Gods. Did she have to do this now, when he was too weak to resist her, when he knew by all rights he should let her go? "That's the imprint talking." His words came out harsher than he intended.

"No, dammit, it's not!" She fisted her hands by her side. "Look. I've never been the kind to fall in love. Lust, yes. But never love. I know—" she thumped herself in the chest with her balled up little knuckles "—I know I love you. I just don't want to be a vampire. It's not only an imprint anymore. And if you're too pigheaded to admit you love me, too, then that's not something I can overcome with test tubes and scientific method."

Achilles turned away, unable to bear the hurt in her eyes any longer. The imprint was strong, making her feel things, think things, she never would have otherwise. Returning to her mortal form was for her own good. He'd always known that.

Beck returned to the lab and stalked back and forth across the room, furious at herself and him. Her heart thumped and ached deep in her chest. Beck stopped, patting herself down and held her hand over her sternum. Good grief. She had a heartbeat! When had that happened?

She stumbled to the nearest lab stool and collapsed on it. There had always been the chance that working with Vanquish would turn her back into her mortal form. She'd fully expected that repercussion. But if she had a heartbeat, then how in the world had she transported back to the lab?

Beck held her hand out in front of her and focused on phasing a cup of hot Earl Grey tea into her hand. She felt the weight and heat of the mug in her fingers before she opened her eyes. She still had her vampire powers! Or were they hers?

Perhaps, just as she'd predicted, the imprint was still

in place and as strong as ever. Perhaps she was just accessing Achilles's vampire powers. The difference was—she knew how to use them, when as a mortal, she hadn't.

Beck gasped, the cup falling to the floor, as her hands went to cover her mouth. The hot tea splashed across the floor as the mug bounced and rolled.

She was still connected to Achilles. If she was in the midst of the transition, then one of two things was happening right now. Either he was transitioning, just as she was and was once more a whole vampire, or he was nearly dead.

Beck shot to her feet, grabbed the latest version of the antidote from the rack where it had been resting along with a new syringe and focused with all her might to take her back to Achilles's side.

She held the antidote tightly in her hand. Achilles lay still, unmoving, his eyes shut. "Achilles?" she whispered. She touched him, then quickly drew her fingers back at the shock of his cool skin. Too cold. Her heart beat faster, harder than it ever had before. His hold on existence was tenuous at best. The spark she'd felt by touching him was now nothing more than a faint friction.

Focusing with everything she had within in her she tried to reach his mind. *Achilles. Wake up. I'm here with you. I have the antidote. Wake up!*

A faint moan issued through his cracked lips. Beck started at the sound, her hands gripping the edge of his bed. Her fingers shook as she took a syringe from her pocket and filled it with the antidote, then blindly searched for a vein in his arm to inject it. With no pulse it was nearly impossible. But she finally found a spot and began to inject the serum.

Beck gasped as she felt herself being transported. *No. Not now!* She held on to Achilles not knowing who was taking her or where she was going.

She found herself sprawled on her knees, Achilles's limp body beside her in a dark field of damp grass. A half moon, cleaved in two just like her heart, hung in the cold air. Her breath came in small pale puffs, as the cold knifed into her lungs.

Blinding pain shot through Beck's skull as her hair was viciously yanked backward, making her back arch unnaturally. Holding her hair was Eris, her blue eyes so cold they glittered like chips of ice. "This isn't over yet."

"Don't you touch him!" Beck scraped her fingernails against the woman's hand prying and digging to release her hair. The blonde was incredibly strong.

Her brittle malicious laugh echoed loudly in the cold air as if it had been broadcast into a microphone making Beck's stomach shrivel in fear. Her voice shifted, reverberating and powerful as her body shifted, growing taller, broader until she was a nine feet tall, her hair writhing as if it had a life force of its own. Beck had never seen anything like it.

Eris's face glowed with dark triumph. "Are you afraid, little mortal? You should be!" She inhaled the air and smacked her lips in satisfaction.

Beck covered Achilles's limp body with her own. "If you're going to take him, then take me, too."

"Do you know who I am?"

Beck nodded her head, but that didn't stop the dark goddess from crowing.

"I am Eris, goddess of discord. If I let him die, then how could I possibly enjoy more of his suffering? Of course he'll live," she spat. "But you, you will suffer for the rest of your days. You'll suffer knowing that he never truly wanted you and desired you to go back to being mortal so he'd be free of you. You'll suffer knowing that you gave up on an eternal bond that could have saved you both centuries of regret and rebirth. You'll suffer, my little mortal, because in the end you'll know you gave up every chance you had at being with the man you loved, just to be mortal again."

Beck looked down at Achilles's pale face, his profile so still it could have been carved of marble, and wept. Eris's laugh echoed long after she'd vanished in a cloud of black mist.

Beck wasn't sure how long she lay there, holding Achilles in her arms. But the bone deep ache and searing pain had begun to subside. Perhaps she was becoming numb to it. Perhaps half of her was already dead, or dying, just as he was.

She stared up at the bright points of starlight in the sky above until the blackness crowding around the edges of her vision blotted out everything.

Chapter 19

Beck awoke, her face wet with dew. The pale light of dawn rimmed the edge of the trees beyond the field, a low fog clinging to the cold earth.

She sat up and blinked, putting a hand to her head as her vision swam. Glancing in the half light, she caught a glimpse of pale skin beside her. Achilles lay in the grass, still as stone.

Beck scrambled to her knees, grabbed handfuls of his shirt and shook him. "Achilles! Achilles! Wake up!"

Eyes closed, his head lolled to the side. He didn't answer. Oh, God. Was he dead? *Really* dead?

Cold beneath her hand, his shirt was as damp as the blades of grass around him. Her heart was beating hard from the adrenaline spiking through her system, swelling and throbbing in her throat. But then, for just a few seconds, shock stopped it. Just when Beck thought it might not beat again, it did. And boy did it hurt.

Worse than sitting beside her father when his lips turned blue as the heart attack claimed him when she was twelve. Worse than being told her mother had died while she was in college, only to discover later that she'd been turned into a vampire by her latest boyfriend and she'd never see her again.

She'd not let herself love after that because it had always ended badly. She should have known better.

Beck lay her head down upon his chest, tears flowing free and hot into his shirt. Great sobs clutched at her chest and she couldn't seem to find enough air to fill the lungs that had gone unused for several weeks.

The ache inside hurt so badly that she almost didn't notice the fingers gently stroking the hair back from her temples. She stilled instantly, holding her breath.

With caution, she opened one eye a fraction and was greeted by the green gaze of the man she loved looking back at her.

He tried to speak, his words little more than a grating rasp she couldn't interpret.

"Achilles? Say it again." Beck scooted closer, leaning her ear close enough to his lips that she could feel his words.

"I'm not dead, sweetling, merely undead," he whispered.

Her heart flipped then double thumped. She laughed, a nervous giggle that bubbled up from inside. It was fantastic. It was impossible. And it made her want to sprout wings and fly. Tears were still streaming down her face. Harder now. But the reason had completely changed.

Achilles had survived.

"You're back!" She grasped his face between her hands and kissed him fiercely. His hand cupped her head, as he threaded his fingers through her hair. The strength of his kiss grew to match her own as he sat up, pulling her into his arms.

The damp wetness of their clothes began to steam in the chilly early morning air. They explored one another with the frantic fury of long-lost lovers. It didn't matter that she was mortal and he was vampire. All that mattered was that they had both survived. An affirmation that despite everything, love could and would prevail. The distinct *flick* of his fangs coming out didn't even faze her. She welcomed them as evidence of his desire as he kissed her.

It felt strange not to feel the pressure build and throb behind her gums as it was doing between her thighs. His hands slipped beneath her clothes sampling the texture of her skin, his thumb grazing the arch of her nipple as he tested the weight and feel of her breast in his palm. Beck leaned into his touch. Craving it. Needing it. She gasped at the sparks shooting through her.

His tongue traced the seam of her lips, stroking, gliding, tasting. Showing her exactly what he'd like to do to her. She broke their kiss, lungs aching for air, lips tender from the press of his fangs against her mouth. "I thought I'd lost you," she panted.

"Never, sweetling." He crushed his mouth to hers as he twisted his body, laying her down in the grass. Achilles pulled back, tracing his fingers tenderly across her face. He brushed the pad of his thumb against her swollen lips, making them tingle.

Beck wanted him to kiss her again. Just like that. Like everything in the universe depended on that kiss alone to hold it together.

"As much as I want you, we have to be careful. You're mortal again, and I don't want to hurt you."

Beck nibbled at her tender lip. "About that. I've decided that I don't want to be mortal after all."

His brows drew together. "Why?"

"I want to be with you. Now. Forever. Always. And I can't do that if I'm mortal, now can I?"

His mouth twisted into a heartbreaking grin. "No. You can't."

Beck combed her fingers through his damp, silky hair, drawing his face back to her. She turned her head, baring her throat. "Be my maker."

"Do you really understand what you're asking of me?" he demanded harshly.

She cupped the back of his stubborn head, tugging his mouth closer to the life's blood throbbing beneath the surface of her skin. "Is it really so different than being my imprinted mentor?"

He resisted the pull, even though Beck felt the hard ridge of his arousal against her thigh, and knew that his fangs must be aching to finish what she'd started. Close. So close.

"It seals the imprint," he warned, his arms tightening involuntarily around her. "It won't matter if we're parted three thousand years from now. You'll always be able to find me, and I'll be drawn to you. You'll always hear my thoughts and feel my power as part of your own. Being your maker only makes an imprint more powerful."

"And what if I don't care?"

"You should."

"What if I want that with you?"

"How can you—"

She pressed her fingers to his lips. "Trust me, I know."

His kiss was one of pure joy and Beck let it infuse her. She pulled back unable to resist teasing him.

"As my mentor you've been remiss about one part of my education."

"Really?"

"You never told me how to make a vampire."

"Ah. Yeah, didn't think you'd really want to know as it involves the giving and taking of blood and ichor. I know how much you dislike blood."

Beck swatted at him.

"And as much as I'd love to give you that particular lesson right now, we've got something more important to do."

A bit of disappointment nibbled away at her glow of happiness. She really hadn't thought he'd balk at her request. Of course she hadn't counted on his drive to do his duty no matter what. But that was one of the things she loved best about him.

"Let me guess. We need to save the vampire world from Eris's vaccine."

"You got it, Doc." He stood up and then reached out to pull her up from the ground and into the circle of his arms. "Ready to fly?"

"As long as we go together."

The familiar suck and pull of transport had a certain comforting quality to it as she held Achilles close, burying her face in his chest, absorbing everything of him she could. They landed back at the clan's medical center, just outside the locked door to her lab. She knew she couldn't do this alone. Screwing together every bit of mortal focus she could muster, she called out to the vampires she knew she could trust.

"You're the only one with the combo, Doc."

Beck reached out and tapped in the security code, and as she did so, the hallway filled with dark particles. Six familiar vampires took shape. Good. She'd been crossing her fingers hoping they'd respond. Hoping that her ability to tap into Achilles's power was still viable.

She glanced at Achilles. "I took the liberty of calling your security team, Dmitri and Kris. I think I may know how we can get this distributed."

Beck led the troop of massive male vampires and her best friend into the white lab and stared for a second at the tan puddle of spilled tea on the floor, now gone cold. She phased away the mess, glad she had reached Achilles when she had.

On the countertop sat the dozen vials of the antidote she'd managed to create.

"We found out which facilities were manufacturing the vaccine and wiped out whatever was in process. But we couldn't stop the distribution of the vaccine completely," Titus reported.

Beck stared at the vials. Did she have enough? What if she could use the very powers that the virus sought to destroy to make more?

"Achilles?"

"Yeah, Doc?"

"If you have a small sample of the antidote, do you think you could phase it into a larger portion?"

"I don't see why not. As long as it exists, it can be replicated, or increased."

"Then I have an idea. Achilles and Kris, you'll be production. I'll pipette a small amount of the antidote into each of the vials, and you phase the rest of it until the vial is full. You five—" she glanced at the security team members and Dmitri "—will distribute the antidote."

"How do we know where to go first?" James asked.

Dmitri swiveled around looking at the security team members. "Go to the clans in the areas where the vaccine went out to the public first. Then make sure every clan in the country has a supply. We want to grant access to every vampire that needs the antidote."

"One thing before we get started." Beck rolled up her sleeves and grabbed a set of syringes and one of the vials. "I need to inject each of you as a precaution."

They worked through the daylight hours and into the night, until they were exhausted. Considering how close Achilles had been to death, Beck was astounded at his resilience. Sixteen hours of constant phasing and transporting was enough to sap the strength of even the most virile vampire.

Beck grinned as she watched Kris lock on to Dmitri with a big hug. "We did it. I think we got it all out in time," said Kris as she turned toward Beck. "Not bad for a mere mortal."

"Pfft," Beck huffed. "Just because I'm mortal doesn't mean I can't bring it." As proof, Beck tapped into Achilles's powers via her imprint and phased in a round of ice cold beers on a tray. "I think our accomplishment calls for a little celebrating."

Kris grinned. "Absolutely." She grabbed Beck in a big enthusiastic hug. "By the way, a little bat told me that you've been reconsidering your stand on remaining mortal."

Beck's gaze flicked to Achilles who shrugged and took a long draw from his beer, green eyes inscrutable. Imprint or no imprint, would forever even be possible if he didn't truly love her?

Kris bumped into her shoulder. "He didn't have to say anything. I can still smell the imprint between you. You two are made for each other."

Beck couldn't resist the magnetic effect he had on her. She walked over to Achilles and he put an arm around her. "I can see where being a vampire might have a certain appeal," she said.

He leaned in and kissed her soundly. Titus and Slade wolf whistled, while James, Mikhail, Dmitri and Kristin cheered. But deep inside, Beck still had her doubts.

She knew she loved the man, the vampire, beside her, but did he feel the same about her? Was it truly just the imprint drawing them together as he'd said? Doubt collected uncomfortably in the pit of her stomach, and Beck pulled away from Achilles. Perhaps she was expecting too much. Love wasn't always a two-way street.

Dmitri stiffened, his face turning serious as he phased away the drink in his hand. "Hold up. It's not time to celebrate just yet. The council wants a report. Now."

Beck shoved her hands through her hair, tired, elated and most definitely feeling the drag of exhaustion like a heavy wool blanket around her shoulders.

"You stay here. I'll be back in half an hour," Achilles ordered.

"I think I've earned the right to be there," Beck fired back.

"Mortals don't go before the council."

Kristin cleared her throat. "I beg to differ. When I went the first time, I was still mortal. And I'm with Beck. She's earned the right to be there."

Achilles's gaze connected with Dmitri's. Instinctively Beck knew there was communication going on between the two of them, but she could no longer hear it. She resisted the surge of disappointment.

She didn't realize how quickly she'd come to rely on her vampire powers, which were no longer hers to command. All she could do was tap into Achilles's powers through the link of their imprint.

She tapped Achilles on the shoulder, then lifted herself up on tiptoe to whisper in his ear. "Is there any time for us to clean up first?"

A rush of warm air blew over her and Beck realized he'd phased away her stained lab coat and rumpled dirty clothes, leaving her shower fresh and in a clean pressed skirt suit.

"Better?"

Beck grinned. "You're good."

"Let's see if you still think that after we make it through the meeting with the council."

He grasped her about the waist and transported them together to the familiar dark doors. They entered the council chambers, but only Roman was present.

Dmitri, Achilles and Beck stepped up onto the dais facing Roman. No one said anything. Maybe they were waiting for Roman to speak first.

"I have been in contact with the lairds of the other clans and our king. They are most pleased with efforts of the Cascade Clan to assist them. You have done well."

"Thank you, my Laird," Dmitri said as he bowed his head in deference to the head of the clan.

"However, *Trejan*, it remains that we have a unique issue at hand. Vanquish is still in circulation, and despite the antidote Dr. Chamberlin formulated so success-fully—" he nodded in her direction "—the rules of our world have permanently changed. Vampires are no longer locked into this existence once the choice has been made. Our security is at risk. Those, such as Dr. Chamberlin, who have been accepted into our clan complex, and then later return to their mortal form can reveal our deepest secrets to the mortals. We must take steps to eliminate this risk."

"Or you could take the risk and give people free choice," Beck pointed out calmly.

Roman's eyes darkened. "You do not know what you are asking for, Dr. Chamberlin."

Everything she'd experienced over the last month about what it meant to be vampire and what it meant to be imprinted made Beck bold. "Actually, I think I do. A year ago, people didn't even know vampires existed. Six months ago if the vampire virus got you, you turned vampire no matter how it had happened. Yesterday, vampires learned that the very thing that gives them their powers could also be used to make them mortal again. What you really have to ask yourself, my Laird, is if you can stop change."

"We have been the same for thousands of years."

"Yes, but eventually everything evolves or disappears. Change is unavoidable. Perhaps it's time for vampires to evolve again, my Laird."

Roman rubbed his bottom lip with his finger, the silence becoming a living, breathing thing within the rock walls of the chamber. Finally he pinned her with his dark gaze. "You have a point, Doctor."

"My Laird." Rebecca glanced at Achilles. His gaze encouraged her. "There is one more thing. My mother was changed some time ago. Is there any way I could locate her with your assistance?"

Roman steepled his fingers. "She may have remained

isolated out of fear of changing you. Are you sure she wishes to be found?"

Beck shook her head. "I don't know, but I'd at least like to try. I want her to know that she can go back to being mortal, if she wants to."

Roman's eyes glittered. "And what of you, Doctor? What are your intentions?"

"My Laird, I'd like to become vampire permanently," she responded.

Roman eyed Achilles. "And are you willing to serve as her maker?"

Achilles pulled back his shoulders, drawing him up so straight and stiff, he looked more like a warrior than she'd ever seen him. "Given our imprint, my Laird, I think I'd have to kill any other vampire that touched her in such an intimate way."

Roman grunted. "Your imprint is strong already. Are you certain you're willing to seal it for eternity?"

"If that is what she wishes."

"Then you have my permission—" he smiled "—and my blessing."

Achilles dipped his head in a bow, giving the familiar salute of his forearm and fist over his chest. "Thank you, my Laird."

"From the smell of it, my blessing is rather an afterthought. Your imprint is already far stronger than any I've encountered in several centuries."

Beck's skin heated with a blush. Achilles's face swiveled in her direction so fast she gasped. The look in his eyes was purely predatory. *Gods, I've forgotten how exquisite your blood smells,* he said in her head.

Roman bit back a grin. "You are free to go."

Beck grabbed Achilles's hand and didn't wait to be told twice. She transported them using the imprint. When the stretch and pull finally subsided, she fully intended for them to be in her bedroom, but found herself somewhere quite different.

"Since you were tapping into my powers I took over our destination. Hope you don't mind the detour." His breath was rough and warm against her hair.

The light of a gibbous moon, now more than half complete, slanted in luminescent shafts through a row of massive fluted white marble columns, casting the floor of the Doric style temple in patches of light and dark.

A warm breeze, laced with the salty tang of the sea and touched with the greenness of rosemary, rippled sheer swaths of fabric that fell like curtains from massive stone beams above the columns to enclose a huge bed covered in crimson silk. Their roof was the dark expanse of night sparkling with stars and the low hanging moon. Two enormous braziers warmed the air and suffused a gentle glow of firelight against the fluted columns. The ancient open-air temple, with the white stone the only part remaining from millennia of exposure, echoed with the shush of the waves outside.

Beck marveled at it all. "Where are we?"

"We're where it all started." He lifted her up into his strong arms and carried her toward the bed, set like an altar in the middle of the temple. "I did a few minor modifications. It's fallen into ruin in the past 2,500 years, but the stone has remained. As has our imprint."

Her heart jumped, not just with surprise or wonder, but with a jolt of recognition. This felt right. He felt right. "I've always wanted to visit Greece."

"There's only one way to really do it justice." He phased away their clothing, leaving them clad only in the fragrant night air.

He set her upon the bed like a precious offering. The cool silk beneath her warmed instantly with the rush of heat pouring through her. Beyond the columns, the moonlight painted a sparkling path on the water, and turned the edges of the waves pearlescent on the shore.

Achilles phased a dark red rose. The heady perfume filled the air as he traced it slowly down her forehead, her nose, then lingered on her mouth. The delicate softness of the petals brushed her lips and sent shivers coursing through her as he began to repeat the course of the rose with his mouth, scattering kisses across her skin, so light, so tender, they were like the faint silken brush of a feather. Teasing, making her skin ache for more.

He lingered at her mouth, his lips first teasing, then more insistent. Sweet and reverent as he was, she wanted more. No, she wanted all of him. Now.

Her hands curved over the round of his strong shoulders and across the muscled planes of his back, drawing him down to her. Every tantalizing inch where bare skin met bare skin sparked into a electrical connection that shimmed through her, making her feel truly alive for the first time. Beck arched up, pressing her aching breasts against him, crushing her mouth to his.

Achilles resisted the urge to take all of her in one mind-blowing rush. Instead he nuzzled her ear, inhaling the vibrant scent of ginger that clung to her hair and the softer, more subtle scent that branded her as his and his alone. His fingers traced beneath the soft curve of her breast, feeling the rapid thumping of her heartbeat just beneath her ribs. She gasped, the sound making him all the harder.

Her excitement became his own, the steady thrum of her mortal blood like the endless rush of the ocean called to him, made him ache with need. There just at the juncture of her neck and collarbone lay the sweet offering. He watched her pale moon-kissed skin throb erratically with the shifting surge of her life's blood.

His fangs extended and there was no holding them back. "Rebecca, before I change you—"

Her soft chuckle vibrated through the wall of his chest, rubbing her against him with a delicious friction. She wrapped a silky leg around his hip and slid downward in a caress. "Go ahead. I already heard you."

"You can still hear me?"

She turned her head to the side, her chestnut curls spilling across the pillow in a dark wave, exposing even more of herself to him. His fangs throbbed, venom pearling at the tips. Achilles wiped away the venom with his tongue, and laved a trail from her ear to the softest spot near her artery as his hands cupped her breasts. She bucked beneath him.

"What are you waiting for?" she gasped. "Do it."

He sunk himself into her, the rush of heat and life pouring into him, through him. She moaned, soft and deep, writhing against him, the heat of her skin searing in its intensity.

Unable to stop himself, he gripped the curve of her sweet derriere, cradling himself against her, damp with perspiration and feminine desire. He stroked along her cleft with his shaft. Exquisite torture for them both.

"Achilles," she moaned his name and he had no defenses. He sunk into her tight wet heat, letting it close around him, strip him of his will, his strength to do or be anything without her. What good was immortality, when you had to be without the one thing that made you whole?

He pulled back, then pressed forward, the delicate slide of her around his shaft a caress he felt to his very core. In their shared mind he experienced her release building, a wave ready to crest with nothing to hold it back.

It shook them both. He arched back with the power of it, crying out her name.

Her rapid breath fanned his face, with the sweet mortal warmth. Inside need warred with knowledge. She'd lose that again. Lose the heartbeat that pounded so steady and sure beneath those lovely breasts. And she'd lose so much more.

But how he needed her. Not just tonight. But forever.

She still had the choice. She had to know what she stood to lose before he would change her. If she still wanted to be a vampire, then and only then, would he complete the maker's process with her.

"Am I a vampire yet?" she asked her eyes sparkling in the moonlight.

He brushed aside a dark curl stuck to her eyelashes with his finger. "That was feeding and fabulous sex. To make you a vampire I have to replace your mortal blood with my ichor."

She skimmed her fingertips over his back, making his skin tighten in response, the desire for her filling him again.

"There is something else you need to know before I can show you how to make a vampire the old-fashioned way."

"What?"

"You need to understand what you're giving up." He lifted himself on an elbow and curved his other arm around her waist, turning her so that her bare bottom pressed against his groin. "Look out at that shore," he whispered into her ear.

"It's beautiful."

"As a vampire you'll never spend a day out on that beach under the warmth of the full sun."

"No more SPF 30? I can live with that."

"You'll lose all those friends and family that are mortal and watch them grow old and die." She shifted, against him, her skin growing cooler, her discomfort scenting the air with the sour hint of vinegar.

"I've already lost almost everyone I've loved."

Her words hit him in the chest like an arrow, piercing his heart. He tenderly caressed her hair with his fingers.

Beck turned to him, looking into his eyes and the pain and loss he saw buried deeply there, as images from her mind flashed into his own, almost broke his heart. She'd suffered so much for such a young mortal.

He kissed her lightly, reaching out to take her hand. "You also won't have children, Rebecca. Vampires only reproduce by making other vampires, and it's against our laws to make a child into one of our kind." Beneath his forearm her stomach tightened reflexively.

"Have you ever wanted children?"

He tore his gaze away from her, staring far out into the ripples of the ocean.

"I never expected to live long enough to have any."

Beck watched the play of the moonlight on his face. His thoughts flitted in and out of her mind. He'd been far too young, too full of Spartan pride at being a great warrior to consider what he stood to lose. And he didn't want her to regret her choice.

She pressed her palm to his cheek and Achilles's gaze connected with hers. "All I've ever wanted was to love and be loved for who I am. To matter more than anything else to someone. I've found that in you."

Achilles looked deeply into her eyes and a wave of something far more potent than desire crashed into her, washing over her and filling in all those bruised, dented spots in her heart. "I love you, Doc. Pure and simple. Just as you are."

A surge of hope welled up inside her, but she held it back. He'd been so certain before that her emotions had been only the imprint. What if that was true for him? "Is that the imprint talking?" she whispered as she touched his sculpted lips.

"Hell, no." He said it so fiercely she felt the words pierce her fingertips.

"How can you be so sure?"

This time he didn't answer. He drew her to him, his eyes mesmerizing in their intensity, and kissed her so deeply Beck felt every pore open, each little hair raise with a static electric effect, drinking him in.

"I've never been more sure of anything in two millennia. You complete me."

"Your better half?" she teased.

"You can say that again, sweetling."

"I have a better idea." *Why don't you kiss me?*

His mouth curved into a devilish smile, his fangs glinting white in the moonlight, and he did just that.

Epilogue

Two things had happened the night Achilles had taken her to the temple, both of them unexpected. One, she had not become a vampire as she'd anticipated because, two, well, perhaps three, she'd conceived that night and was pregnant with twins.

Somehow the antidote had done more than just keep Achilles from turning to dust. In modifying the DNA structure, Beck had inadvertently changed the genetic sequencing that kept vampires sterile. For now the news about the antidote's unexpected side effect was being kept under wraps until she knew exactly what the outcome was going to be. The council had thought it would be best not to stir a panic among the clans until they were secure in knowing how to explain the facts to others of their kind.

One thing scared Beck more than becoming a vampire all over again, and that was becoming a parent. With Roman, Dmitri, Kris and Achilles's help, she'd found her mother among a nest of reivers on the East Coast. Victor or Vane, or whatever he had called himself over the centuries, had twisted her mind so much from the person Beck use to think of as her mother, that she hardly recognized Beck when they'd finally met.

They'd resumed a rocky relationship, and it made Beck all the more insecure about what kind of parent she'd be. Nevertheless, Beck kept counting down the days until she could return to being a vampire.

"You're certain we have to wait?" They lay spooned together in the center of their king-size, four-poster bed. Light from the candles filtered through the sheer silk canopy.

Judging by how she felt, the day was nearly over. Being mortal on a nocturnal schedule was proving to be less of a challenge than she'd anticipated. But it was necessary since they were living in their apartment in the clan complex.

Achilles kissed her on the forehead. "Do you want to argue another round with Dr. Shepperd?"

Beck sighed and snuggled closer to him, letting the firm warmth of him curve around her backside. "No." But the waiting was agonizingly slow.

Achilles smoothed his hands along her full belly and Beck felt the babies twirl and roll in response to their father's touch. "Oooo, no, no, baby, not there." She pressed gently at the tiny foot lodged just beneath her rib until it released.

"They're just as eager to arrive as you are to hold them in your arms."

"I don't think so." She turned to look at her mate, a flutter of panic kick-starting her heart.

The pillow shifted as he cocked his head to the side. "What's wrong?"

"What if they're born mortal?"

The lines furrowing his brow smoothed out as he spiraled one of her brown curls around his finger. "Then we watch them grow, and if they decide to become vampires, we become their makers."

"But what if they're born vampire?"

"Then we'll learn along with everyone else how that works."

"What if they have only one fang?"

He brushed a soft tender kiss along her temple, then rested his unshaved cheek against her. "We will love them anyway. If you keep worrying like this, you'll age far more than you ever planned on before we can change you back into a vampire."

Beck sighed, stuffing the big body pillow wedged under her enormous stomach into a more comfortable position.

"Turning back into a vampire isn't going to repair the stretch marks, is it?"

He nuzzled her ear. "I'm afraid I'm the wrong person to ask about those sort of things."

"I'm ready to be done."

"Patience, sweetling."

Patience, I don't think so. She was tired of being the size of a small, okay, large, limousine. Even when she sat down her belly extended just over the tips of her knees. A sharp pain speared across her lower back, gripping her belly, making it hard. Beck sucked in a startled yelp, then let out her breath as slow and even as she could manage as the pain subsided.

Achilles stared at her in horror. "What was that?"

Beck arched her eyebrows. "*That* was a labor pain."

She wasn't certain if he'd feel what she did when it came to labor because of their imprint.

Achilles sat up looking at his mate, eyeing her warily. "That can't be right. Are you certain it is supposed to hurt that much?"

"You want the good news or the bad news?"

"Bad."

"They'll get closer together."

He winced. "Good?"

"They'll end after the babies are born."

And when exactly was that supposed to be? An audible *pop* sounded and their gazes connected. "What was that?"

"I think my water just broke."

Achilles didn't waste any time, he grabbed a towel from their bathroom, trying to help Rebecca clean up as he tried to reach the doctor through his mind.

Let me know when the pains are less than five minutes apart, Dr. Shepperd responded.

They get that close?

Actually, they'll crest into one another before the birth.

Achilles gripped the edge of the table as he and Rebecca groaned together.

You better come now.

The wall of pain crested, tearing him in two like a pair of chariot horses tied to either end of him, then prodded to take off in opposite directions. Achilles arched with the pain.

As a Spartan, he'd been whipped, he'd been beaten, he'd walked for days without food and only the merest supply of water. But never, never had he endured such as this.

The only time he'd ever come close is when they'd tortured Ione. Panic seized him, making his throat swell shut even as the pain began to recede.

"Don't you dare die on me," he growled at Rebecca.

Her tightly closed eyes snapped open. The pointed glare could have ignited a match. "I'm not dying. It's called labor. You just wish you were dead." Sweat dotted her skin, making her hair curl even more tightly. "You'd better call Dr. Shepperd while you still can. They're coming fairly close together."

"Already did," he muttered through clenched teeth as pain radiated through him.

A spiral of dark smoke curled in the room. Achilles thanked the gods Dr. Shepperd was so quick, but his thanks came too soon. The dark particles knit together in the form of Dmitri's wife, Kristin, as she transported into their bedroom.

"How exciting!" She clapped her hands together. "The babies are coming." She hurried over to Rebecca and grasped her friend's hand. "How are you doing?"

"We're in labor. How in the hell do you think she's doing?" Achilles snarled.

Kristin looked up, flipping her long blond hair behind her shoulder. "Nice of you to be so supportive."

Another column of smoke appeared as Dr. Shepperd arrived. "How's our mother faring?" He smiled.

Achilles panted, barely able to stand. "Do something! We— *She's* in pain!"

Dr. Shepperd stared at him for a moment, his eyebrow arching over the edge of his wire-rimmed glasses. "Interesting."

For the next two hours Achilles did everything he could to stifle the pain, trying to put all his focus on Rebecca. As the latest wave of pain passed he lay panting, drenched in his own sweat. "How's she doing?" he managed between quick breaths he didn't even need to fill his lungs.

"Better than you," came Kristin's arch reply.

Another contraction caught him up in the tidal wave of pain. His body struggled against itself, and he could feel muscle fiber tearing in his groin, a fire so intense it felt like a red hot metal sword searing his flesh. He cried out.

"The baby's head is cresting. That's good, keep going, Rebecca. Push." She let out a hard low cry that cleaved through him.

Then there was release. Blessed total release. The

room rang with the lusty cry of a set of newborn lungs. His whole body melted into a puddle unable to move.

"You've got a fine baby boy." Dr. Shepperd cradled the infant for a moment before handing him off to Kristin to hold.

"Oh, gods, he's gorgeous. Look at that dark hair," she cooed.

Achilles barely had time to sit up before he was knocked to the mattress again with the same searing fire.

"Time for round number two," the doctor said, far too calmly.

The raw screaming pain escalated and he and Rebecca shouted out together.

"There it is. Push!" the doctor encouraged.

And then, just like before, the intensity of the pain was matched by a flood of adrenaline that created total release. A second cry echoed to join the first.

"A beautiful girl!"

Achilles swore every bone in his body was liquefied. His eyes were shut, but he sensed the warm, squirming bundle that was placed in his arms.

He opened his eyes and stared down at the impossibly little person. The small pink lips, full and damp, opened in a cry, pink little toothless gums peeping out. Dark hair swirled over the tiny head no bigger than his fist.

He placed the knuckle of his pinky against the little questing mouth and the cry stopped as the baby suckled. "I think this one's hungry."

"May I?" the doctor asked as he lifted the tiny bundle

and transferred it to Rebecca's breast. "I'll be back to check on you both in a few hours."

Achilles didn't miss how Dr. Shepperd nudged Kristin with his arm. "Um, yeah. I'm going to go tell Dmitri the good news. One of each. How cool is that?"

They both disappeared in a cloud of dark particles. Achilles was glad they were finally gone. He turned to look at Rebecca. She was more than his wife. She was his mate, his other half. A fierce joy filled him as he watched the tiny babies feed one after the other at her breast.

Using the last ounce of energy he possessed, he phased his bed right beside Rebecca's and curled one of the sleeping babies between them.

"Look, I think we have a little vampire," she murmured softly.

Achilles watched as Rebecca unlatched the nursing infant and lifted the baby's lip to show minute twin fangs poking out from the smooth gumline.

"So when did you want me to make you a vampire?"

She kissed him lightly, nibbling at his lip, making him growl low where heat stirred in his belly.

"I think we're going to have to wait until I'm done nursing."

"Why?"

"Listen."

He listened intently. There were three human heartbeats in the room, one lower and slower, two fast and light. He looked up into her sparkling eyes. "It's impossible."

"Improbable, not impossible."

"But they have fangs."

"And yet part of them is still human. We can't take the chance that they'd survive on blood alone."

He nodded. "You're right. We'll wait. But only until they're weaned. I'm not taking a chance of losing you."

She kissed him soundly, her fingers curling into the hair at his nape, making him fire with longing for her. She broke their kiss and he shook his head, chuckling. "Living vampires. It's like you told Roman, everything changes."

Rebecca smiled at him in a way that sunk in deep and grabbed hold of his heart in a way he wanted to enjoy for eons to come. "No, not everything," she said softly, inching in closer for another kiss.

Achilles traced his fingers along the edge of her face, memorizing every line, loving the woman beside him and knowing he'd be with her for all time. "Then name me one thing that never changes."

She grinned. "Love."

* * * * *

nocturne™

COMING NEXT MONTH

Available June 28, 2011

#115 VACATION WITH A VAMPIRE...
AND OTHER IMMORTALS
Maggie Shayne and Maureen Child

#116 NIGHTWALKER
The Nightwalkers
Connie Hall

You can find more information on upcoming
Harlequin® titles, free excerpts and more at
www.HarlequinInsideRomance.com.

HNCNM0611

REQUEST YOUR FREE BOOKS!

2 FREE NOVELS PLUS 2 FREE GIFTS!

n○cturne™

Dramatic and Sensual Tales of Paranormal Romance.

YES! Please send me 2 FREE Harlequin® Nocturne™ novels and my 2 FREE gifts (gifts are worth about $10). After receiving them, if I don't wish to receive any more books, I can return the shipping statement marked "cancel." If I don't cancel, I will receive 4 brand-new novels every other month and be billed just $4.47 per book in the U.S. or $4.99 per book in Canada. That's a saving of at least 15% off the cover price! It's quite a bargain! Shipping and handling is just 50¢ per book in the U.S. and 75¢ per book in Canada.* I understand that accepting the 2 free books and gifts places me under no obligation to buy anything. I can always return a shipment and cancel at any time. Even if I never buy another book, the two free books and gifts are mine to keep forever.

238/338 HDN FC5T

Name	(PLEASE PRINT)

Address	Apt. #

City	State/Prov.	Zip/Postal Code

Signature (if under 18, a parent or guardian must sign)

Mail to the **Reader Service:**
IN U.S.A.: P.O. Box 1867, Buffalo, NY 14240-1867
IN CANADA: P.O. Box 609, Fort Erie, Ontario L2A 5X3
Not valid for current subscribers to Harlequin Nocturne books.

Want to try two free books from another line?
Call 1-800-873-8635 or visit www.ReaderService.com.

* Terms and prices subject to change without notice. Prices do not include applicable taxes. Sales tax applicable in N.Y. Canadian residents will be charged applicable taxes. Offer not valid in Quebec. This offer is limited to one order per household. All orders subject to credit approval. Credit or debit balances in a customer's account(s) may be offset by any other outstanding balance owed by or to the customer. Please allow 4 to 6 weeks for delivery. Offer available while quantities last.

Your Privacy—The Reader Service is committed to protecting your privacy. Our Privacy Policy is available online at www.ReaderService.com or upon request from the Reader Service.

We make a portion of our mailing list available to reputable third parties that offer products we believe may interest you. If you prefer that we not exchange your name with third parties, or if you wish to clarify or modify your communication preferences, please visit us at www.ReaderService.com/consumerchoice or write to us at Reader Service Preference Service, P.O. Box 9062, Buffalo, NY 14269. Include your complete name and address.

HN11

USA TODAY *bestselling author B.J. Daniels takes you on a trip to Whitehorse, Montana, and the Chisholm Cattle Company.*

RUSTLED

Available July 2011 from Harlequin Intrigue.

As the dust settled, Dawson got his first good look at the rustler. A pair of big Montana sky-blue eyes glared up at him from a face framed by blond curls.

A woman rustler?

"You have to let me go," she hollered as the roar of the stampeding cattle died off in the distance.

"So you can finish stealing my cattle? I don't think so." Dawson jerked the woman to her feet.

She reached for the gun strapped to her hip hidden under her long barn jacket.

He grabbed the weapon before she could, his eyes narrowing as he assessed her. "How many others are there?" he demanded, grabbing a fistful of her jacket. "I think you'd better start talking before I tear into you."

She tried to fight him off, but he was on to her tricks and pinned her to the ground. He was suddenly aware of the soft curves beneath the jean jacket she wore under her coat.

"You have to listen to me." She ground out the words from between her gritted teeth. "You have to let me go. If you don't they will come back for me and they will kill you. There are too many of them for you to fight off alone. You won't stand a chance and I don't want your blood on my hands."

"I'm touched by your concern for me. Especially after you just tried to pull a gun on me."

"I wasn't going to shoot you."

Dawson hauled her to her feet and walked her the rest of the way to his horse. Reaching into his saddlebag, he pulled out a length of rope.

"You can't tie me up."

He pulled her hands behind her back and began to tie her wrists together.

"If you let me go, I can keep them from coming back," she said. "You have my word." She let out an unladylike curse. "I'm just trying to save your sorry neck."

"And I'm just going after my cattle."

"Don't you mean your boss's cattle?"

"Those cattle are mine."

"*You're* a Chisholm?"

"Dawson Chisholm. And you are…?"

"Everyone calls me Jinx."

He chuckled. "I can see why."

Bronco busting, falling in love…it's all in a day's work.
Look for the rest of their story in

RUSTLED

Available July 2011 from Harlequin Intrigue
wherever books are sold.